Experimental Research in
The Psychology of Music: 9

Studies in the Psychology of Music
Volume 9

EDWIN GORDON

General Editor

Experimental Research in
The Psychology of Music: 9

EDWIN GORDON

Editor

UNIVERSITY OF IOWA PRESS 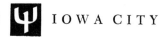 IOWA CITY

Library of Congress Catalog Card Number: 73-632181
University of Iowa Press, Iowa City, Iowa   52242
© 1974 by The University of Iowa. All rights reserved
Printed in the United States of America
ISBN 87745–048–X

CONTENTS

PREFACE

Nearly half a century ago, Carl E. Seashore initiated the Studies in the Psychology of Music at The University of Iowa. Dean Seashore was astutely aware of the need for furthering experimental research in the psychology of music, and the publication of the series represented only one of his major contributions to this cause.

The immediate overwhelming acceptance of the Studies in the Psychology of Music has not diminished over the years in spite of the fact that the series had to be discontinued in the 1930s. It is with great respect for the visionary genius of Carl E. Seashore that I am carrying forth his work and have accepted the responsibility of reactivating the Studies in the Psychology of Music some twenty years after his death. The support of my professional colleagues in recognizing the particular importance of the dissemination of results of current experimental research studies in the psychology of music provided impetus for the publication, in 1967, of Volume V of the series and for the following collection of articles which constitutes Volume VI.

Under the aegis of The University of Iowa, the Studies in the Psychology of Music will be published annually. It is anticipated that because of the interdisciplinary nature of the psychology of music, each yearly volume will comprise a set of experimental research studies bearing on music, education, psychology, measurement, and/or acoustics. Undoubtedly, the continued success of the series is in large part dependent on the extent to which worthy studies are contributed for publication.

Edwin Gordon

A STUDY OF ABILITY IN SPONTANEOUS AND PREPARED JAZZ IMPROVISATION AMONG STUDENTS WHO POSSESS DIFFERENT LEVELS OF MUSICAL APTITUDE

Joseph James Briscuso

PURPOSE OF THE STUDY

The past two decades have been most important for jazz education in the public schools, and the impact of jazz has brought about changes in both general music and instrumental music curriculums. Since 1958, the number of jazz bands in the schools has grown to more than 8,000.[1] Furthermore, the success of these performing groups has been such that the idea of young people playing big band jazz is now generally accepted by the academic community.

Within recent years, increased emphasis has been placed upon the problem of relevance in education. Music educators have not been exempt from these challenges directed toward the traditional curriculum. In July 1969, the question of a relevant approach to music education came to the fore at the Youth Music Institute in Madison, Wisconsin. The University of Wisconsin Extension Music Department, the United States Office of Education, and the Music Educators National Conference were the co-sponsors of the month-long discussion of the question. This inquiry prompted the following statement by M.E.N.C. President, Wiley L. Housewright:

> Church choirs, marching bands, choruses, and orchestras do not fully satisfy the musical appetites of the young . . . . thousands of American youth want more. . . . Young people's music can be held at bay outside the institutions of society as it largely is at present, or it can be recognized as a vital and welcome new regenerative force and invited to assume a respectable position in the American musical culture. . . . There is much to be gained from

---

Joseph James Briscuso is Director of Bands at Wheaton Warrenville High School, Wheaton, Illinois.
[1] Paul O. Tanner, "The Musical Values of the Stage Band," *Music Educators Journal* 51 (April–May 1965):83.

the study of any musical creation. Rock, soul, blues, folk, and jazz cannot be ignored. . . . The Music Educators National Conference . . . not only accepts rock and other present-day music as legitimate, but sanctions its use in education.[2]

True, relevance is a word that has become a cliché in educational philosophy. Yet, one cannot overlook the fact that many traditional notions are being challenged. As a result, many educators are engaged in curriculum developments that hopefully represent a positive response to today's known demands and to the yet unspecified needs of the future.

To the present time, there have been no experimental research studies related to the teaching of jazz improvisation. Moreover, whereas the *Musical Aptitude Profile*[3] is known to possess validity in regard to its use in typical school music endeavors,[4] no one has investigated the possibility that the scores derived from the test battery could aid music teachers in adapting instruction in jazz improvisation to students' individual needs. Also, there is little evidence regarding which tests, if any, could be used to identify the students who, following a period of instruction, would exhibit the greatest (or least) talent in jazz improvisation. Therefore, the specific problems of this study were:

1. To determine whether students classified as "high," "average," or "low" on the *Musical Aptitude Profile Tonal Imagery* test reveal differences in their mean scores on measures of improvisational skill; to consider the same question with regard to students classified according to these same aptitude levels on (a) the *MAP Rhythm Imagery* test, (b) the *MAP Musical Sensitivity* test, and (c) the *MAP* composite test. Implicit in this, of course, was the desire to determine whether mean differences on improvisational measures are clearly larger for levels constituted on the basis of any one of the aptitude tests than on the others.

2. To examine the level-to-level trend in mean improvisational skill for two different types of improvisation: that involving musical material prepared in advance and that demanding a more spontaneous performance. When, as in this study, spontaneous and prepared performances are con-

---

2 Wiley L. Housewright, "Youth Music In Education," *Music Educators Journal* 56 (November 1969):45.

3 Edwin Gordon, *Musical Aptitude Profile* (Boston: Houghton Mifflin, 1965).

4 Edwin Gordon, *A Three-Year Longitudinal Predictive Validity Study of the Musical Aptitude Profile,* Studies in the Psychology of Music, vol. 5 (Iowa City: University of Iowa Press, 1968); and Edwin Gordon, "Taking Into Account Musical Aptitude Differences Among Beginning Instrumental Students," *Experimental Research in the Psychology of Music,* Studies in the Psychology of Music, vol. 6 (Iowa City: University of Iowa Press, 1970), pp. 45–64.

sidered "treatments" (to use the terminology of experimental design), the presence of an interaction between treatments and levels may be explored. This issue was considered separately for each aptitude test.

An interaction would occur if the mean differences (in improvisation) from level to level were relatively large for one type of performance and relatively small (or zero) for the other type. An alternative way in which interaction might manifest itself would be for the two improvisation means to be very similar for high aptitude students but farther apart for the lower aptitude students. In some educational settings—and possibly in this one—the two treatment conditions could show the reverse trend. The largest difference could occur for the high aptitude group and progressively smaller differences could arise for lower aptitude groups. Any such level-to-level variation in the size of the mean difference (spontaneous vs. prepared) represents an interaction.

METHODS AND PROCEDURES

Members of the jazz bands of Iowa City High School, Iowa City, Iowa, Mount Vernon High School, Mount Vernon, Iowa, Southeast Junior High School, Iowa City, Iowa, and West Branch High School, West Branch Iowa, served as subjects in this investigation. In all, the experimental sample numbered forty-eight students. This total included seven eighth-grade students, seventeen ninth-grade students, seven tenth-grade students, thirteen eleventh-grade students, and four twelfth-grade students. Although none of the subjects had previous experience or training in jazz improvisation, a minimum of three years instrumental training was a prerequisite to participation in the study.

In October 1970, all students were given *MAP* prior to any instruction in jazz improvisation. The test was administered in one session at each school, and an attempt was made to provide the best possible testing conditions. Students who were absent and missed taking one or more parts of *MAP* were tested later on an individual basis.

The instruction which constituted a control element in this study centered on a nonrequired course entitled "Jazz Improvisation." All instruction was provided by the investigator. Classes met in each school as an extracurricular activity for a two-hour period each week for thirty weeks. The general objective of the course was to develop improvisational facility that would demonstrate students' ability to play with jazz style. The goal of the course was to teach students to perform extemporaneously "theoretically correct" jazz improvisations.

The content of individual class meetings was not structured to deal only with improvisation. At least one-half of each class meeting was devoted to playing jazz band arrangements. In this way, the students became more aware of jazz style and interpretation. The remaining portion of each class meeting was spent in teaching the theoretical principles used in jazz, in developing improvisational facility, and in developing the students' ability to analyze and evaluate jazz solos. At all times, emphasis was placed on learning to play with jazz style.

A necessary part of this experiment was the development of a course of study for a first-year student studying jazz improvisation. In addition, materials were developed to guide and assist the teacher in teaching such a course. Included in these materials were exercises in rhythmic and melodic ear training, and six "play along" arrangements of jazz compositions with sections where the students might improvise.

Procedure for Gathering the Data

The criteria for evaluating each student's ability in jazz improvisation were based on two performances: (1) a tape-recorded performance of a thirty-two measure pop-song[5] in the concert key of B♭ Major, and (2) a tape-recorded performance of a twelve measure blues in the concert key of F Major. The same selections were utilized for the spontaneous and the prepared improvisations of the pop-song and the blues.

The pop-song *Doggin' Around*, composed by E. W. Battle and H. Evans, and *The München, 19km., Blues*, composed by the writer, were chosen as criteria compositions for this investigation. The difficulty levels of these selections correspond, in general, to that of the music which was used in group lessons during the school year. Furthermore, the technical demands of each selection were comparable for all instruments. It was expected, therefore, that the criteria compositions would provide ample opportunity for each student to demonstrate whatever ability he had achieved.

Each student's performance of the criteria compositions was tape-recorded by the investigator in May 1971. The spontaneous performances of the pop-song and blues were tape-recorded during the third to last class meeting. The prepared performances of the pop-song and blues were tape-recorded during the final class meeting. The interjacent week was devoted to review and preparation of the criteria compositions.

In order to relieve undue apprehension on the part of the students, the

---

[5] The term "pop-song" will be employed to denote a popular style composition with an AABA formal outline.

purpose and procedure of the recording sessions was discussed prior to the recording of any performances. The recording equipment was arranged in an unobtrusive manner and ample time was allowed to record the performances. The pop-song performances were recorded first and the blues performances second. All recording was done at 7½ IPS on one side of high-fidelity tapes. Each student was identified by the numerical order of his performance on each of the several numbered tapes.

The evaluation of the tape-recorded performances was accomplished independently by three judges: a faculty member of the School of Music of The University of Iowa, a faculty member of the School of Religion of The University of Iowa, who is also a prominent local jazz musician, and a musician who is teaching music at another institution. The evaluation was based on the following aspects of each performance:

a. harmonic awareness
b. rhythmic development and interest
c. melodic expressiveness
d. ability to play with jazz style
e. individuality

The quality of each student's tape-recorded performances was evaluated on the basis of the following rating scale:

	Excellent	Above Average	Average	Below Average	Poor
	5	4	3	2	1
Harmonic awareness					
Rhythmic development and interest					
Melodic expressiveness					
Ability to play with jazz style					
Individuality					

Thus, using the above rating scale, each of the three judges assigned five ratings for the spontaneous pop-song improvisation, five ratings for the spontaneous blues improvisation, five ratings for the prepared pop-song improvisation, and five ratings for the prepared blues improvisation. The sum of these five ratings constituted the total score assigned by each judge for each of the four improvisations. Therefore, the total score awarded by a single judge on any particular improvisation could range from a minimum of five points to a maximum of twenty-five points. The "improvisation totals" awarded by each judge were then summed to obtain a composite score for each of the four improvisations. A composite score for each of the four improvisations could range from a minimum of fifteen points to a maximum of seventy-five points.

Statistical Design and Analysis

For the purpose of this study, a two dimensional "mixed" design of the kind Lindquist refers to as a Type I was employed. This treatments-by-levels-by-subjects design is diagramed below:

	Spontaneous Improvisation	Prepared Improvisation
High **MAP**		
Average **MAP**		
Low **MAP**		

The "treatments" in this study were the two methods of performing jazz improvisation, i.e., spontaneously or after preparation. Each student musician was evaluated under both treatments. The levels dimension was determined on the basis of scores obtained on the *Musical Aptitude Profile*.

The effects of particular interest which were tested for significance were: (1) the interaction[6] between treatments and levels, (2) the main effect of treatments,[7] and (3) the main effect of levels.[8] The .05 level of confidence was used to determine the significance of the attained F values.

The analysis was conducted eight times. Four of the analyses involved the pop-song performances. The *Tonal Imagery* scores were used for the first analysis, the *Rhythm Imagery* scores were used for the second, the *Musical Sensitivity* scores for the third, and the *MAP* composite scores were used for the fourth analysis. Similarly, the second set of four analyses involved the blues performances, with each of the four *MAP* scores serving in turn as the levels variable.

RESULTS

Establishment of *MAP* Levels

At the outset of the semester, *MAP* was administered to all students who participated in the experiment. Total scores on each of the three main divisions of the test battery (*Tonal Imagery, Rhythm Imagery, Musical Sensitivity*) and on the composite score for the complete battery were derived.

For the purpose of this study, it was decided that the three aptitude levels (high, average, and low) should contain equal numbers of students. That is, for each *MAP* score, the sixteen highest scoring students were designated as the high *MAP* group, the sixteen lowest scoring students were defined as the low *MAP* group, and, the remaining sixteeen student scores were taken as the average *MAP* group.

For the *Tonal Imagery* test, the highest level students scored above the 94th percentile; the lowest level included students who scored below the 70th percentile; and students who scored between the 71st and the 93rd percentiles were included in the group having average tonal aptitude. For the *Rhythm Imagery* test, the top third included students who scored above

---

6 The interaction test concerns the constancy of the differences between treatments (spontaneous versus prepared) from level to level (high *MAP*, average *MAP*, and low *MAP*). A lack of significant interaction is interpreted as a failure to demonstrate that the differences between treatments vary from level to level.

7 A test of the main effect of treatments (spontaneous versus prepared) bears on the presence or absence of a difference for all levels combined.

8 A test of the main effect of levels concerns the presence or absence of a relationship between *MAP* test scores and criterion scores at all levels.

the 89th percentile; the lowest third included students who scored below the 71st percentile; the middle third of the students scored between the 72nd and 88th percentiles. For the *Musical Sensitivity* test, students who were designated as having high expressive aptitude scored above the 86th percentile; students were designated as having low expressive aptitude if they scored below the 57th percentile; students who scored between the 58th and 85th percentiles were designated as having average expressive aptitude. For the composite *MAP* test, the top level included students who scored above the 93rd percentile; students who scored below the 71st percentile were designated as having low over-all musical aptitude; and students who scored between the 72nd and 92nd percentiles were designated as having average over-all musical aptitude.

Because of the selectivity of the experimental subjects and the use of one-thirds to define levels, students who ranked as high as the 93rd percentile were, necessarily, treated as having average musical aptitude. Similarly, students who ranked as high as the 71st percentile were treated as having low musical aptitude. Thus, the designations "high," "average," and "low" have a restricted meaning in this study and do not conform to a more general use of these terms.

Comparison of Students' Achievement in Spontaneous and Prepared Jazz Improvisation by Aptitude Levels

Means and standard deviations for the spontaneous and prepared performances, level by level and over-all, are presented in Table 1. The analysis of variance for the spontaneous and prepared performances is presented in Table 2.

It can be seen that none of the interaction tests resulted in a statistically significant ratio. Thus, within the arbitrary designations of levels of musical aptitude assigned to students in this study, the data provide no conclusive evidence that the level-to-level trend for prepared performances differed from that for spontaneous performances. To state the same finding in another way, the difference between means for spontaneous and prepared performances did not vary significantly from one level to another.

In a creative area such as jazz improvisation, one might expect that the difference between individuals at the extremes of the aptitude continuum would be more apparent in prepared than in spontaneous material. With additional preparation time, the musician with superior talent should develop more artful, creative modes of expression. Moreover, good instruction in music, like good instruction in most fields, should magnify this difference; it should equip the potentially able performer to realize his poten-

[8]

Table 1
Means and Standard Deviations of Spontaneous and Prepared Improvisations Using MAP Scores for the Levels Dimension
(N = 48)

MAP Scores		N	Pop-Song						Blues					
			Spontaneous		Prepared		Mean	Over-all	Spontaneous		Prepared		Mean	Over-all
	Level		Mean	S.D.	Mean	S.D.	Diff.	Means	Mean	S.D.	Mean	S.D.	Diff.	Means
Tonal Imagery	High	16	49.3	9.34	53.9	7.11	4.6	51.6	51.5	6.50	55.3	8.39	3.8	53.4
	Average	16	48.3	7.85	49.9	7.78	1.6	49.1	48.3	8.38	53.9	7.95	5.6	51.1
	Low	16	45.0	6.76	47.6	4.18	2.6	46.3	48.9	4.95	53.1	6.26	4.2	51.0
	Over-all	48	47.5		50.5		2.9	49.0	48.9		53.1		4.5	51.8
Rhythm Imagery	High	16	45.9	9.05	51.1	8.21	5.2	48.5	47.5	5.27	52.3	7.65	4.8	49.9
	Average	16	49.0	5.74	51.1	5.15	2.1	50.1	49.6	6.66	54.8	6.92	5.2	52.3
	Low	16	47.7	9.21	49.2	7.23	1.5	48.4	49.5	8.52	52.3	8.71	2.8	50.9
	Over-all	48	47.5		50.5		2.9	49.0	48.9		53.1		4.3	51.0
Musical Sensitivity	High	16	49.4	8.00	53.8	6.35	4.4	51.6	52.1	6.53	57.1	6.48	5.0	54.6
	Average	16	48.9	8.63	52.1	7.31	3.2	50.5	50.2	7.11	54.9	7.73	4.7	52.5
	Low	16	44.2	7.03	45.7	4.15	1.5	44.9	44.5	4.85	47.4	5.82	2.9	46.0
	Over-all	48	47.5		50.5		3.0	49.0	48.9		53.1		4.2	51.0
Composite	High	16	48.1	9.71	52.7	7.31	4.6	50.3	49.8	6.22	54.3	7.44	4.5	52.1
	Average	16	49.7	7.10	52.0	7.53	2.3	50.8	50.8	8.38	55.4	8.60	4.6	53.1
	Low	16	44.8	6.87	46.9	4.34	2.1	45.9	46.1	5.17	49.7	6.23	3.6	47.9
	Over-all	48	47.5		50.5		3.0	49.0	48.9		53.1		4.2	51.0

Table 2

Analysis of Variance F-Ratios of Spontaneous and Prepared Improvisations Using *MAP* Scores for the Levels Dimension

(N = 48)

	Source of Variation	df	Pop-Song	Blues
Tonal Imagery	Subjects			
	Levels	2	2.29	1.97
	Within Subjects			
	Treatments	1	11.53*	24.54*
	Interaction	2	0.97	0.79
Rhythm Imagery	Subjects			
	Levels	2	0.26	0.46
	Within Subjects			
	Treatments	1	11.86*	24.48*
	Interaction	2	1.66	0.74
Musical Sensitivity	Subjects			
	Levels	2	4.74*	8.94*
	Within Subjects			
	Treatments	1	11.52*	24.30*
	Interaction	2	0.96	0.57
Composite	Subjects			
	Levels	2	2.56	2.67
	Within Subjects			
	Treatments	1	11.42*	23.85*
	Interaction	2	0.75	0.14

* Significant at the 55% level. $F_{.05} (1,45) < 4.05$. $F_{.05} (2,45) < 3.20$

tial and also, it should enable him to take advantage of the time allowed to develop and refine good musical ideas. Given this reasoning, the failure to find such differences in trends (interaction) is somewhat disappointing. However, it is possible that the lack of interaction may lie in the homogeneity of the levels groups.

As can be seen in Table 2, the main effect of treatments is statistically significant at the .05 level for all analyses. The observed mean differences (see Table 1) at each of the three aptitude levels consistently favor the prepared performances. Therefore, while there is no evidence to suggest that students with high musical aptitudes are better able to benefit from instruction in jazz improvisation than students with average and low musical aptitudes, the data do provide evidence that, with additional specific instruction, all students, regardless of aptitude levels, are able to improve their improvisational performance.

[10]

Finally, in regard to the main effect of levels, it can be seen in Table 2 that this effect is not statistically significant in the analyses involving the *Tonal Imagery* test, the *Rhythm Imagery* test, or the *MAP* composite test. Thus, the data provide no evidence of a relationship between the level of these *MAP* test scores and criterion scores. In contrast to the previous findings, however, the analyses involving the *Musical Sensitivity* test, also reported in Table 2, reveal that the main effect of levels is statistically significant. This important finding shows that there is a relationship between students' *MAP Musical Sensitivity* scores and their subsequent degrees of achievement in spontaneous and prepared jazz improvisation. This is not surprising in that the three subtests included in the *Musical Sensitivity* total test are the only musical preference tests in the *MAP* battery. The S_1 and S_3 tests are designed to assess interpretative ability; the S_2 test is designed to indirectly assess creative ability. Therefore, it appears that musical expression and musical creativity, as measured by *MAP*, are related to the art of improvisation. It may be, therefore, that the *MAP Musical Sensitivity* test may serve a specific function to indicate this relationship.

The absence of a statistically significant main effect of levels in the analyses involving the *Tonal Imagery* test, the *Rhythm Imagery* test, and the *MAP* composite test may be due to any of several possibilities. It is possible that improvisation abilities draw upon aptitudes somewhat different from those measured by these three sections of the *MAP* battery. That is, from these data, the potential implied by *Tonal Imagery*, by *Rhythm Imagery* or by the *MAP* composite tests, does not predict significantly the ability to improve creative improvisations. Because of the narrow range among aptitude levels in this homogeneous grouping, it is possible that, if the students had displayed as great a range of aptitude in the areas of *Tonal Imagery* and *Rhythm Imagery* as in *Musical Sensitivity*, the two former tests, like that of *Musical Sensitivity* would have shown a significant effect. Further, factors which could have prevented the demonstration of statistically significant interaction among levels might be related to the validity of the evaluative criteria or from the nature of the judges' ratings. It is conceivable that some misunderstanding contributed to differences among judges' ratings, or that the judges may not have been consistent in their emphasis upon specific qualities of performance. Too, a seven-point rating scale, for example, might have been more efficient and effective for discriminating subtle aspects of the musical performances than was the five-point rating scale. (The rather low paired judges' reliability coefficients presented in Table 4 are consistent with these possibilities.)

The means and standard deviations of the ratings awarded by individual judges for the pop-song and blues performances are presented in Table 3. It can be seen that the observed mean ratings for the prepared performances are, with one exception, higher than the mean ratings for the spontaneous performances. The one exception is the pop-song performance means reported for Judge Three.

It may be noted that the observed mean ratings awarded by Judge Two are consistently higher than those of Judge One. Also, Judge Three, with one exception, recorded ratings that average higher than those of Judge One and Judge Two. The exception involves the high mean (19.52) for Judge Two on the prepared blues performances.

The correlations between ratings of the judges are presented in Table 4. These correlations may be interpreted as inter-judge reliability coefficients.

Table 3

Means and Standard Deviations for Students' Spontaneous and
Prepared Pop-Song and Blues Performances by Individual Judges
(N = 48)

| | Pop-Song | | | | Blues | | | |
| | Spontaneous | | Prepared | | Spontaneous | | Prepared | |
	Mean	S.D.	Mean	S.D.	Mean	S.D.	Mean	S.D.
Judge 1	14.41	3.98	14.91	3.28	14.88	2.97	15.54	3.19
Judge 2	15.02	2.82	17.52	2.44	16.44	2.31	19.52	2.89
Judge 3	18.08	3.29	18.00	2.81	17.60	3.28	18.27	3.28

Table 4

Reliability Coefficients of Judges' Ratings
of Students' Tape-Recorded Performances
(N = 48)

| | Paired Reliability Coefficients | | | |
JUDGES	Spontaneous Pop-Song	Prepared Pop-Song	Spontaneous Blues	Prepared Blues
1–2	.55	.62	.44	.73
1–3	.48	.58	.66	.56
2–3	.48	.48	.49	.69
	Pooled Reliability Coefficients			
1–2–3	.74	.79	.77	.85

The reliability of the composite score for all ratings combined on each type of performance is also presented in Table 4.

It can be observed that the reliabilities for a single judge, as indicated by the correlations for the pairs, are comparatively low. They range from a low of .44 to a high of .73. However, when the reliabilities of all three judges are pooled, the coefficients increase. They range from a low of .74 to a high of .85.

Summary of the Results

The separate treatments-by-levels-by-subjects analyses of variance for each of the two criteria compositions revealed no significant interactions. However, the main effect of treatments, which favored prepared improvisation, was found to be statistically significant for all analyses.

The analyses involving the *Tonal Imagery* test, the *Rhythm Imagery* test, and the *MAP* composite test revealed no statistically significant main effect for levels. However, the main effect of levels was found to be statistically significant in the analyses involving the *MAP Musical Sensitivity* test.

CONCLUSIONS

Experience in teaching jazz improvisation in conjunction with this study has led the author to believe that instrumental improvisation can be taught. The average scores obtained in this experiment (generally above 3.4 on a "per judgment" basis) represent a level well above that which students demonstrated (informally) at the start of the experiment. Consistent with this subjective judgment is the experimental evidence which indicates that student performance does improve when several days are available to develop and refine musical ideas.

However, the results of this study failed to provide consistent, convincing evidence that after one year of instruction the improvisation skills of those with *MAP* aptitude levels above the 90th percentile reach a higher level than those who possess somewhat lower levels of musical aptitude. Only for the *Musical Sensitivity* test was such a relationship to aptitude level demonstrated. Nor could it be shown that those with the highest aptitude level used several days of preparation time to greater advantage than did those in the lowest aptitude level. Nonetheless, the hypothsis that aptitude factors account for some of the differences in improvisational skill cannot be ruled out on the basis of this study. However, factors other than *MAP* aptitudes are possibly more potent.

[13]

BIBLIOGRAPHY

Gordon, Edwin. *A Three-Year Longitudinal Predictive Validity Study of the Musical Aptitude Profile.* Studies in the Psychology of Music, vol. 5. Iowa City: University of Iowa Press, 1967.

————. *Musical Aptitude Profile.* Boston: Houghton Mifflin, 1965.

————. "Taking Into Account Musical Aptitude Differences Among Beginning Instrumental Students." *Experimental Research in the Psychology of Music.* Studies in the Psychology of Music, vol. 6. Iowa City: University of Iowa Press (1970):45–64.

Housewright, Wiley L. "Youth Music in Education." *Music Educators Journal* 56 (November 1969):45.

Lindquist, Evert F. *Design and Analysis of Experiments in Psychology and Education.* Boston: Houghton Mifflin, 1965.

Tanner, Paul O. "The Musical Values of the Stage Band." *Music Educators Journal* 51 (April–May 1965):83–84.

AN INVESTIGATION OF THE EFFECT OF THE PROVISION OF THE "IN DOUBT" RESPONSE OPTION ON THE RELIABILITY AND VALIDITY OF CERTAIN SUBTESTS OF THE IOWA TESTS OF MUSIC LITERACY

Roger V. Foss

Multiple-choice tests are a popular means of evaluation of achievement. Some reasons for their popularity are the objective scoring, the high reliability, and the possibility of assessing many aspects of achievement in a relatively short period of time. However, many test users question the appropriateness of multiple-choice procedures because of the possibility of guessing the correct answer and the frustration that students may experience when they have no basis for making a choice.

A technique used to discourage guessing and minimize frustration is to give students the opportunity to state frankly their lack of knowledge through the use of an "in doubt" response. The "in doubt" response option is provided in the *Metropolitan Achievement Tests*,[1] the *Musical Aptitude Profile (MAP)*,[2] and in all of the *Aural Perception* and *Reading Recognition* subtests of the *Iowa Tests of Music Literacy (ITML)*.[3]

Three studies have dealt with the appropriateness of the "in doubt" response option. They are: "A Study of the *Musical Aptitude Profile*," by Florence Reusch Culver,[4] "An Investigation of the Interrelation of Personality Traits, Musical Aptitude, and Musical Achievement," by Stanley Schleuter,[5] and "An Investigation of the Interrelation of Personality Traits,

Roger V. Foss is an associate professor of music at Wiley College, Marshall, Texas.

[1] Walter N. Durost, et al., *Metropolitan Achievement Tests* (New York: Harcourt Brace Jovanovich, 1970).

[2] Edwin Gordon, *Musical Aptitude Profile* (Boston: Houghton Mifflin, 1965).

[3] Edwin Gordon, *Iowa Tests of Music Literacy* (Iowa City: Bureau of Educational Research and Service, Division of Extension and University Services, University of Iowa, 1970).

[4] Florence Reusch Culver, "A Study of the *Musical Aptitude Profile*" (M.A. thesis, University of Iowa, 1965).

[5] Stanley Schleuter, "An Investigation of the Interrelation of Personality Traits, Musical Aptitude, and Musical Achievement." *Experimental Research in the Psychology of Music:8*, Studies in the Psychology of Music. vol. 8 (Iowa City: University of Iowa Press. 1972).

Musical Achievement, and Different Measures of Musical Aptitude," by Robert W. Thayer.[6]

Culver's study, which included an investigation of the effect of the "in doubt" response on the validity of *MAP*, revealed higher criterion-related validity when the "in doubt" response option was provided. The other two studies, which dealt primarily with the relationship between specific personality traits and the incidence of use of the "in doubt" response on *ITML* (and not with more direct validity factors), revealed no systematic associations. Therefore, in an attempt to derive additional pertinent information, the problem of this study was to investigate the effects of the provision of the "in doubt" response option on the reliability and validity of selected subtests of the *Iowa Tests of Music Literacy.*

DESCRIPTION OF THE *IOWA TESTS OF MUSIC LITERACY*

The complete battery of *ITML* consists of six Levels. Each Level, comprised of six subtests, is divided into two sections: *Tonal Concepts* and *Rhythmic Concepts,* with three identically titled subtests in each section— *Aural Perception, Reading Recognition,* and *Notational Understanding.* The subtests, which are designed to measure parallel concepts at each Level, become more complex from Level 1 through Level 6. *ITML* Levels 1, 2, and 3 may be appropriately administered to students in grades four through twelve. Levels 4, 5, and 6 are recommended for students in grades seven through twelve.

The four types of tonality[7] included in the *Tonal Concepts* subtests of *ITML* are major, minor, modal, and unusual. Of the modes which suggest tonality, the test author refers to major and harmonic modes as "usual" modes. The dorian, phrygian, lydian, and mixolydian modes, because of their less frequent use, are referred to as "unusual" modes. According to Gordon, some tonal patterns bear no functional relationship to any mode, and as a result, any tonality which they might suggest is a matter of subjective opinion. He refers to these nontonal patterns as "unusual" tonality.[8]

---

6 Robert W. Thayer, "An Investigation of the Interrelation of Personality Traits, Musical Achievement, and Different Measures of Musical Aptitude," *Experimental Research in the Psychology of Music:8,* Studies in the Psychology of Music. vol. 8 (Iowa City: University of Iowa Press. 1972).

7 "Tonality" implies music which gives "loyalty to a tonic," as defined by Willi Apel. *Harvard Dictionary of Music,* 2d ed. (Cambridge: The Belknap Press of Harvard University Press, 1969. p. 855.

8 Edwin Gordon. *Iowa Tests of Music Literary Manual* (Iowa City: Bureau of Educational Research and Service. The University of Iowa. 1970). p. 9.

The tonalities used in each Level of *ITML* are outlined in Table 1.

The four types of meter included in the *Rhythmic Concepts* subtests of *ITML* are duple, triple, mixed, and unusual. Music which moves in duple meter, such as 2/4, or in triple meter, such as 6/8, is considered by the test author to be in "usual" meter. Music which combines duple and triple

Table 1

Modes and Meters Comprised in Each Level of *ITML*

Levels	Tonality	Meter
1	Major	Duple
	Minor	Triple
2	Major	Duple
	Minor	Triple
3	Usual	Usual
	Modal	Mixed
4	Usual	Usual
	Unusual	Unusual
5	Major	Mixed
	Minor	Unusual
6	Major	Mixed
	Minor	Unusual

meter, that is, which contains triplet figures in duple meter, or duplet figures in triple meter is referred to by Gordon as "mixed" meter. Music written in a meter such as 5/8 or 7/8 is classified as "unusual" meter.[9] The meters used in each Level of *ITML* are also outlined in Table 1.

DESIGN OF THE STUDY

Subjects

Seventh grade students in five junior high schools in or near Iowa City, Iowa, participated in the study. The schools represented were: Southeast Junior High School, Iowa City; University Laboratory School, Iowa City;

---

9 Gordon. *ITML Manual*, p. 10.

Regina Junior High School, a parochial school in Iowa City; and junior high schools in West Branch and Mount Vernon, Iowa. In all, 327 students participated in the study. However, 51 of the students were absent during one or more of the four testing days and they had to be eliminated from the study. Therefore, only 276 sets of usable scores were analyzed.

Testing Procedure

ITML was administered by the author during regularly scheduled general music classes. Only three of the six Levels of *ITML* were used in the study because of limitations of time and subjects. Levels 1, 3, and 5 were selected to represent a wide range of difficulty. Test items in these Levels are comprised of major, minor, and unusual modes and duple, triple, mixed, and unusual meters. The students were administered only the *Aural Perception* and *Reading Recognition* subtests from each section of the specified Level of *ITML*. *Notational Understanding* subtests were not included because they do not contain the "in doubt" option.

Level 1 was administered to one group of 90 students; Level 3 was administered to a different group of 90 students; and Level 5 was administered to a third group of 96 students. Each of the groups of students was administered a given Level of *ITML* two times—once in the standard version and once in an experimental version. The experimental version was identical to the standard version except that the "in doubt" option was eliminated. To eliminate systematic bias, approximately half of each group of students was given the standard version of the *ITML* battery during the first day of testing. During the following class meeting, these students were given the experimental version of that same Level of the tests. Conversely, the remaining half of each group of students was initially given the experimental version of the battery during the first day of testing. During the following class meeting, the standard version of that same Level of *ITML* was administered.

Validity Criterion Measures

After the three groups of students had been administered both versions of the specified Levels of *ITML*, they were asked to demonstrate certain musical understandings and behaviors. Validity criterion measures were developed for each group to correspond with the musical concepts of mode and meter comprised in Levels 1, 3, and 5 of *ITML*. The validity criterion measures were presented in two forms: (1) tape-recorded tests with answer sheets and (2) students' individual performances of etudes. Examples used in these three sets of measures are appended to this paper.

Although test items in *ITML* subtests are comprised of tonal patterns and rhythm patterns heard in isolation (so that tonal patterns involve no rhythm and rhythm patterns involve no pitch), the first form of validity criterion measures was comprised of musical excerpts which embodied both tonal and rhythmic concepts in a musical context. The students were asked to listen to thirty tape-recorded musical excerpts, each of which was about ten seconds in length and which represented various musical styles and periods. First, the students identified the brief excerpts by mode. The same excerpts were then played again for meter identification.

The mode identification portions and the meter identification portions of the validity criterion measures were preceded separately by tape-recorded instructions. The students were instructed to mark their responses on an answer sheet by circling letters which represented the two options provided for mode identification or for meter identification, respectively. The options were the same in each case as those used in the *Aural Perception* subtest for the *Tonal Concepts* and the *Rhythmic Concepts* sections of the appropriate Level of *ITML*, as listed in Table 1. It should be stressed, as indicated on the answer sheet appended to this paper, that the validity criterion measures did not contain an "in doubt" response option.

For the performance measures of the validity criteria, students were given approximately five minutes of training as a class on the four etudes which they were asked to perform. Then, each student performed individually for the test administrator. The test administrator established the tempo and a comfortable pitch level for each of the four etudes for each student. All etudes were performed on the neutral syllable "ta."

The individual performances of the etudes were tape-recorded and later evaluated independently by a music professor, a graduate music student, and the writer. The first two etudes were evaluated for rhythmic accuracy and the last two etudes were evaluated for pitch accuracy according to the following scale:

Poor	Fair	Average	Good	Excellent
1	2	3	4	5

Analysis

The initial analysis involved computation of the means, standard deviations, and reliability coefficients for the Tonal and Rhythmic *Aural Perception* and *Reading Recognition* subtests, the two total tests, and the composite test scores for both the standard and experimental versions of *ITML*.

[19]

Split-halves reliability coefficients, corrected for length through the use of the Spearman-Brown Prophecy Formula,[10] were obtained for each of the *ITML* scores.

The second analysis concerned the means, standard deviations, and reliability coefficients of the mode recognition and meter recognition validity criterion measures. Split-halves reliability coefficients, Spearman-Brown corrected, were obtained for the mode and meter recognition measures.

Means and standard deviations were determined for the performances on the validity criterion etudes by combining the three judges' ratings for each student on each of the four etudes, the combined melodic etudes, the combined rhythmic etudes, and on the combined ratings of all four etudes. Reliabilities were estimated for the performances through interjudge correlations.

The scores on the validity criterion measures for each student were correlated with the scores obtained for the Tonal and Rhythmic *Aural Perception* and *Reading Recognition* subtests, the two total tests, and the composite test scores on both the standard and experimental versions of *ITML*. Also, a "t" test was used to determine if the differences between the corresponding validity coefficients for the two *ITML* test versions were statistically significant at the .05 level.

For theoretical interest, the effect of the test administration sequence on test results was also investigated. Comparisons were made between the validity coefficients for the different versions of the test that were administered first and those that were given second.

Finally, percentages were computed for the number of times the "in doubt" response was chosen in the standard version of *ITML*. Results were computed for those tests that were administered first and for those that were given second to determine if the test administration sequence affected the frequency of use of the "in doubt" response.

PRESENTATION AND INTERPRETATION OF DATA

In order to facilitate reporting the results of this study, the following abbreviations are utilized:

ITML   *Iowa Tests of Music Literacy*
  TC   *Tonal Concepts*
    T–1   Aural Perception

---

[10] E. F. Lindquist, *Design and Analysis of Experiments* (Boston: Houghton Mifflin, 1953), Chapter XVI.

T–2   Reading Recognition

T   *Tonal Concepts*–Total Test

RC   *Rhythmic Concepts*

    R–1   Aural Perception

    R–2   Reading Recognition

    R   *Rhythmic Concepts*–Total Test

C   *Composite Score*

VC   Validity Criterion Measures

    VC–T1   Mode Recognition

    VC–T2   Melodic Performance

    VC–T   Tonal Total

    VC–R1   Meter Recognition

    VC–R2   Rhythmic Performance

    VC–R   Rhythmic Total

    VC–C   Composite Score

Std.   Standard Version

Exp.   Experimental Version

ITML Means, Standard Deviations, and Reliabilities

The means, standard deviations, and reliability coefficients, as reported in Tables 2 through 4, are very similar to those derived from the *ITML* standardization program, as reported by Gordon.[11] However, it should be noted that in the *ITML* Manual, scores for students in grades 7, 8, and 9 are combined for normative purposes. Therefore, test means for the present study are, as expected, slightly lower because they are based on the scores of only seventh grade students.

The means for the experimental version of *ITML* in which the "in doubt" response option was not provided are slightly higher than the means for the standard version of *ITML*. The means range from 49.8 to 55.5 for the experimental version, compared with a range from 45.5 to 53.0 for the standard version. A probable causative factor for this is that when the students were administered the experimental version of the test, they were instructed to guess if they were "in doubt" about the correct answer. Undoubtedly some answers were guessed correctly which resulted in higher means for the experimental version of *ITML*.

Split-halves reliabilities, Spearman-Brown corrected, are higher for the standard version than for the experimental version for all subtests, total

---

[11] Gordon, *ITML Manual*, pp. 100–105.

Table 2

ITML Level 1 Standard Version and Experimental Version Means, Standard Deviations, and Reliabilities

N = 90		Means		Standard Deviations		Reliabilities[*]	
Version		Std.	Exp.	Std.	Exp.	Std.	Exp.
TONAL CONCEPTS							
Aural Perception (T–1)		53.0	55.5	10.37	8.87	.91	.87
Reading Recognition (T–2)		52.9	53.6	11.23	9.32	.86	.75
Tonal Total (T)		53.0	54.5	9.57	7.09	.92	.88
RHYTHMIC CONCEPTS							
Aural Perception (R–1)		49.4	52.9	11.80	11.09	.80	.80
Reading Recognition (R–2)		52.6	53.9	10.06	8.63	.83	.75
Rhythmic Total (R)		51.0	53.4	9.13	7.53	.87	.78
COMPOSITE (C)		52.0	53.9	8.20	6.68	.93	.91

[*] Spearman-Brown corrected.

Table 3

ITML Level 3 Standard Version and Experimental Version Means, Standard Deviations, and Reliabilities

N = 90		Means		Standard Deviations		Reliabilities[*]	
Version		Std.	Exp.	Std.	Exp.	Std.	Exp.
TONAL CONCEPTS							
Aural Perception (T–1)		45.5	49.8	10.70	9.16	.77	.68
Reading Recognition (T–2)		51.7	54.1	11.46	9.99	.84	.77
Tonal Total (T)		48.7	52.0	8.65	7.45	.84	.77
RHYTHMIC CONCEPTS							
Aural Perception (R–1)		47.1	51.4	11.80	8.67	.77	.32
Reading Recognition (R–2)		48.5	51.8	10.63	8.36	.51	.08
Rhythmic Total (R)		47.8	51.7	9.27	6.38	.73	.41
COMPOSITE (C)		48.2	51.8	7.81	5.67	.84	.74

[*] Spearman-Brown corrected.

tests, and composite tests, except for R–1, Level 5, which is .02 lower. And R–1, Level 1, is the same for both versions of the test. Specifically, subtest reliabilities range from .40 to .91 for the standard version, with most co-

Table 4

ITML Level 5 Standard Version and Experimental
Version Means, Standard Deviations, and Reliabilities

N = 96		Means		Standard Deviations		Reli-abilities*	
Version		Std.	Exp.	Std.	Exp.	Std.	Exp.
TONAL CONCEPTS							
Aural Perception (T–1)		51.4	54.4	11.12	10.23	.77	.74
Reading Recognition (T–2)		47.8	53.2	9.00	8.54	.40	.29
Tonal Total (T)		49.7	53.8	8.43	7.38	.79	.65
RHYTHMIC CONCEPTS							
Aural Perception (R–1)		47.5	50.0	9.96	9.14	.77	.79
Reading Recognition (R–2)		47.4	52.0	10.58	7.73	.76	.54
Rhythmic Total (R)		47.5	51.0	8.65	6.81	.85	.80
COMPOSITE (C)		48.5	52.4	7.55	5.95	.90	.82

* Spearman-Brown corrected.

efficients being in the upper .70s and .80s. For the experimental version, the subtest reliabilities range from .08 to .87, with most coefficients being in the .70s. The largest differences between the two test versions were found for the two *Rhythmic Concepts* subtests of Level 3. Apparently, many students were unfamiliar with the difference between usual meter and mixed meter. Thus, when the "in doubt" response option was not provided, guessing occurred, and this probably accounts for the lower reliability coefficients and, as indicated previously, the higher means for the experimental version.

Frequency of the Use of the "In Doubt" Response

For all subtests combined, the "in doubt" response was used approximately seven per cent of the time on Level 1, 10 per cent of the time on Level 3, and 13 per cent of the time on Level 5. Also, on *ITML* Level 1, the "in doubt" response was used more often when the standard version was administered first. The "in doubt" response was used with the same frequency for both administrations on *ITML* Level 3. And, on *ITML* Level 5, the "in doubt" response was used more often when the standard version was administered second. Frequency of use of the "in doubt" response for all subtests, total tests, and composites for the first and second administrations of *ITML* Levels 1, 3, and 5 is presented in Table 5.

[23]

Validity Criteria Reliabilities

The reliabilities for the validity criterion measures that correspond to *ITML* Levels 1, 3, and 5 are reported in Table 6. The reliability coefficients

Table 5

Frequency of Use of the "In Doubt" Response
on *ITML* Levels 1, 3, and 5 When Administered
First and When Administered Second

	T–1	T–2	T	R–1	R–2	R	C
			Level 1				
First	6%	1%	4%	7%	5%	6%	5%
Second	11%	7%	9%	9%	9%	9%	9%
Over-all	8.5%	4%	6.5%	8%	7%	7.5%	7%
			Level 3				
First	14%	6%	10%	8%	13%	10%	10%
Second	12%	7%	9%	11%	12%	11%	10%
Over-all	13%	6.5%	9.5%	9.5%	12.5%	10.5%	10%
			Level 5				
First	14%	13%	13%	17%	17%	17%	15%
Second	11%	11%	11%	12%	12%	12%	11%
Over-all	12.5%	12%	12%	15%	15%	15%	13%

obtained for mode recognition and meter recognition are .77 and .78, respectively, for the measures corresponding to *ITML* Level 1. These reliability coefficients are very similar to the *ITML* subtest reliability coefficients reported in the test manual.[12] The coefficients corresponding to the validity criterion measures for Level 3, however, are only .25 and .02. Although the reason for the low reliabilities is not definitely known, a possible explanation may be that the students had received little training in the recognition of music written in mixed meter and in modes other than major and minor. This is substantiated to some extent by the comparatively low reliabilities for corresponding experimental version *ITML* subtests. Similarly, the validity criterion measures corresponding to *ITML* Level 5 yielded low reliabilities, .29 for mode recognition and .54 for meter recognition. Although these coefficients are higher than the coefficients for the

---

[12] Gordon, *ITML*, pp. 100–105.

validity criteria which correspond to Level 3, they are, nevertheless, considerably lower than the reliabilities reported for the *ITML* subtests. However, the interjudge reliabilities for the validity criterion performance etudes that correspond to all three *ITML* Levels are very high—generally above .90.

Table 6

Validity Criteria Reliabilities
Corresponding to *ITML* Levels 1, 3, and 5

	Validity Criteria Corresponding to		
	Level 1	Level 3	Level 5
VC–T1	.77*	.25*	.29*
VC–T2			
Judge 1 and Judge 2	.89	.87	.92
Judge 1 and Judge 3	.94	.90	.95
Judge 2 and Judge 3	.91	.93	.96
VC–R1	.78*	.02*	.54*
VC–R2			
Judge 1 and Judge 2	.94	.91	.92
Judge 1 and Judge 3	.95	.93	.95
Judge 2 and Judge 3	.96	.93	.94

* Reliabilities for VC–T1 and VC–R1 are Spearman-Brown corrected.

Validity Coefficients

Correlations were computed for students' scores on subtests, total tests, and composite tests for the standard and experimental versions of *ITML* Levels 1, 3, and 5 with each of their measured musical behaviors.

Although all of the correlations are of theoretical interest, only those correlations designed to measure the same trait have practical value for this study. For example, the correlation between *ITML* T–1 and VC–T1 would seem to be of greater concern than the correlation between *ITML* T–1 and VC–R2. Therefore, validity coefficients for each subtest, test total, and composite test for both versions of *ITML* Levels 1, 3, and 5 with only corresponding validity criteria have been summarized in Tables 7 through 9. It can be seen that sixteen of these observed correlations are higher for the experimental version, four are higher for the standard version, and one is the same for both versions of the test.

In order to derive an objective interpretation of observed differences between the validity coefficients reported in Tables 7, 8, and 9, the signifi-

[25]

Table 7
ITML Level 1 Standard Version and Experimental Version
Validity Coefficients

N = 90	Standard Version							Experimental Version							"t" Ratio
	T–1	T–2	T	R–1	R–2	R	C	T–1	T–2	T	R–1	R–2	R	C	
VC–T1	.55							.56							.14
VC–T2		.61							.64						.46
VC–T			.68							.67					.19
VC–R1				.10							.26				1.80
VC–R2					.51							.62			1.35
VC–R						.31							.54		3.24*
VC–C							.55							.67	2.19*

* Statistically significant at the .05 level. The "t" value at the .05 level for 90 df is 1.99.

Table 8
ITML Level 3 Standard Version and Experimental Version
Validity Coefficients

N = 90	Standard Version							Experimental Version							"t" Ratio
	T–1	T–2	T	R–1	R–2	R	C	T–1	T–2	T	R–1	R–2	R	C	
VC–T1	.00							−.09							.75
VC–T2		.52							.45						.91
VC–T			.38							.33					.56
VC–R1				−.06							.06				1.01
VC–R2					.31							.44			1.20
VC–R						.26							.37		1.05
VC–C							.41							.51	1.17

The "t" value at the .05 level for 90 df is 1.99.

Table 9
ITML Level 5 Standard Version and Experimental Version
Validity Coefficients

N = 96	Standard Version							Experimental Version							"t" Ratio
	T–1	T–2	T	R–1	R–2	R	C	T–1	T–2	T	R–1	R–2	R	C	
VC–T1	.29							.31							.23
VC–T2		.27							.37						.87
VC–T			.42							.49					.87
VC–R1				.12							.13				.08
VC–R2					.46							.46			.00
VC–R						.47							.49		.22
VC–C							.50							.61	1.52

The "t" value at the .05 level for 96 df is 1.99.

cance of the differences between the validity coefficients for the two versions of *ITML* were computed. Of the 21 differences, two were found to be statistically significant at the .05 level. The two significant differences were found for the *Rhythmic Concepts* Total Test and the Composite Score for the Level 1 battery.

The fact that the reliability of the standard versions of *ITML* is higher but the validity is lower than the experimental version could be attributed to the method of scoring the tests. It is possible that a weighted scoring procedure might have produced comparatively higher validity coefficients for the standard version.

Effect of Administration Sequence on *ITML* Validity

Comparisons were made to determine if the order in which the standard and experimental versions of the tests were administered affected the validity of the use of the "in doubt" response. Validity coefficients were computed between the *ITML* tests that were administered first and their corresponding validity criterion measures, and also between the *ITML* tests that were administered second and their corresponding validity criterion measures. All correlations are reported in Tables 10 through 12.

It is interesting to note that the validity coefficients are in general higher for the version given first, regardless of whether it was the standard or experimental version. This finding suggests that order of administration of the tests may be as important as the use of the "in doubt" response option to the validity of a test.

CONCLUSIONS

Considering the validity criteria and the standard test scoring procedures used in this study, it may be concluded that the provision of the "in doubt" response option does not increase the over-all validity of a test.

Table 10

Validity Coefficients for the *ITML* Level 1 Standard and Experimental Versions When Administered First and When Administered Second

		T–1		T–2		T		R–1		R–2		R		C	
		Std.	Exp.	Std.	Exp.	Std.	Exp.	Std.	Exp.	Std.	Exp.	Std.	Exp.	Std.	Exp.
VC–T1	First	.56	.63												
	Second	.50	.52												
VC–T2	First			.62	.57										
	Second			.39	.46										
VC–T	First					.70	.73								
	Second					.55	.52								
VC–R1	First							.38	.04						
	Second							−.29	.36						
VC–R2	First									.29	.67				
	Second									.43	.47				
VC-R	First											.33	.45		
	Second											.07	.51		
VC-C	First													.58	.66
	Second													.32	.59

Table 11

Validity Coefficients for the *ITML* Level 3 Standard and Experimental Versions When Administered First and When Administered Second

		T–1		T–2		T		R–1		R–2		R		C	
		Std.	Exp.	Std.	Exp.	Std.	Exp.	Std.	Exp.	Std.	Exp.	Std.	Exp.	Std.	Exp.
VC–T1	First	.04	−.02												
	Second	−.13	−.28												
VC–T2	First			.65	.49										
	Second			.42	.38										
VC–T	First					.49	.27								
	Second					.22	.29								
VC–R1	First							−.22	−.08						
	Second							.12	.18						
VC–R2	First									.49	.40				
	Second									.10	.46				
VC–R	First											.36	.23		
	Second											.19	.47		
VC–C	First													.52	.45
	Second													.30	.50

[29]

Table 12

Validity Coefficients for the *ITML* Level 5 Standard and Experimental Versions When Administered First and When Administered Second

		T–1		T–2		T		R–1		R–2		R		C	
		Std.	Exp.	Std.	Exp.	Std.	Exp.	Std.	Exp.	Std.	Exp.	Std.	Exp.	Std.	Exp.
VC–T1	First	.33	.26												
	Second	.22	.36												
VC–T2	First			.27	.27										
	Second			.26	.49										
VC–T	First					.42	.42								
	Second					.41	.57								
VC–R1	First							.24	−.10						
	Second							.01	.31						
VC–R2	First									.39	.40				
	Second									.51	.59				
VC–R	First											.35	.35		
	Second											.59	.61		
VC–C	First													.42	.54
	Second													.60	.69

Musical Excerpts—Validity Criteria for *ITML* Level 1

Item	Mode	Meter	Composer or Performer and Title
1	m	D	Electric Prunes—"Giant Sunhorse"
2	m	D	Beethoven—Symphony No. 7, Op. 92, "Allegretto"
3	M	T	Vivaldi—Recorder Concerto in C, "Allegro"
4	M	T	Morley—"Sing We and Chant It"
5	M	D	Beatles—"Carry That Weight"
6	m	T	Mozart—"Deh Vieni"
7	M	T	Haydn—Symphony No. 103, "Menuet"
8	m	T	Ars Nova—"Pavan for My Lady"
9	M	D	Bach—Orchestral Suite No. 3, "Bourrée"
10	m	D	Aretha Franklin—"Chain of Fools"
11	M	T	Vivaldi—"Autumn"
12	M	D	Basie—"Taps Miller"
13	m	T	Lumberjack Song—"The Shanty Boys in the Pine"
14	M	T	Mozart—Divertimento No. 8, K.213, "Menuet"
15	m	T	Chopin—Op. 34, No. 2, "Waltz"
16	M	D	Praetorius—"Bourrée"
17	M	D	Bach—"Brandenburg Concerto No. 5" New York Rock and Roll Ensemble
18	m	T	Grainger—"The Lost Lady Found"
19	m	T	Beethoven—Quartet, Op. 18, No. 4 "Menuetto"
20	m	D	Blood, Sweat and Tears—"Sometimes in Winter"
21	M	D	Monteverdi—"Ecco mormorar l'onde"
22	m	D	Bach—Violin Partita No. 1, "Bourrée" Segovia
23	M	D	Bach—"Brandenburg Concerto No. 5" New York Rock and Roll Ensemble
24	m	T	Bizet—L'Arlesienne Suite No. 1, "Carillon"
25	m	D	Cannonball Adderley—"Dat Dere"
26	M	T	Handel—"Water Music"
27	M	T	Menotti—The Shepherds' Chorus, from "Amahl and the Night Visitors"
28	M	D	Brown—"New York Light Guards Quickstep" Goldman Band
29	M	T	Gounod—"Faust Waltz"
30	m	D	Rolling Stones—"Mother's Little Helper"

R1

R2

T1

T2

Musical Excerpts—Validity Criteria for *ITML* Level 3

Item	Mode	Meter	Composer or Performer and Title
1	u	U	Metis—"At the Gate of the Gospel"
2	U	U	Cannonball Adderley—"Dat Dere"
3	U	M	Bernstein—Maria, from "West Side Story"
4	u	M	Barlow—"The Winter's Past"
5	U	U	Bach—"Cantata 140"
6	U	M	Lalo—"Symphonie Espagnole," Op. 21
7	U	M	Grieg—"Piano Concerto in A Minor," Op. 16
8	u	U	Niles—"Jesus the Christ Is Born"
9	U	M	Britten—There Is No Rose, from "A Ceremony of Carols"
10	U	M	Saint-Saëns—"Havanaise"
11	u	U	Niles—"I Wonder as I Wander"
12	U	U	Basie—"Taps Miller"
13	U	U	Grainger—"The Lost Lady Found"
14	u	U	Neidhart von Reuenthal—"Willekommen Mayenschein"
15	U	M	Alfvén—"Midsommarvarka," Op. 19
16	U	M	Gershwin—"Rhapsody in Blue"
17	U	U	Electric Prunes—"Giant Sunhorse"
18	u	U	Fauré—"Prelude No. 6 in E Flat Minor"
19	U	M	Ravel—"Rapsodie Espagnole"
20	u	M	Delibes—Marche de Bacchus, from "Sylvia"
21	u	U	Metis—"Happy to be Home"
22	U	U	Morley—"Sing We and Chant It"
23	U	U	Bach—Violin Partita No. 1, "Bourrée" Segovia
24	U	M	Tschaikovsky—"Symphony No. 5"
25	u	U	Simon and Garfunkel—"Scarborough Fair"
26	U	M	Fauré—"Nocturne No. 4 in E Flat Major," Op. 36
27	u	U	Harris—Folksong Symphony 1940, "Johnny Comes Marching Home"
28	U	M	Nigerian Folk Song—"Saturday Night"
29	U	U	Praetorius—"Bourrée"
30	u	U	English Carol—"God Rest Ye Merry Gentlemen"

R1

R2

T1

T2

Musical Excerpts—Validity Criteria for *ITML* Level 5

Item	Mode	Meter	Composer or Performer and Title
1	M	U	Chávez—"Sinfonia India"
2	M	M	Fauré—"Nocturne No. 4 in E Flat Major," Op. 36
3	m	U	Webber—"Joseph and the Amazing Technicolor Dreamcoat"
4	M	U	Stravinsky—Firebird Suite, "Finale"
5	m	M	Brahms—"Double Concerto for Violin and Cello," Op. 102
6	M	U	Menotti—"The Unicorn"
7	M	U	Ravel—"String Quartet in F Major"
8	M	M	Bernstein—Maria, from "West Side Story"
9	M	U	Brubeck—"Three to Get Ready"
10	m	M	Grieg—"Piano Concerto in A Minor," Op. 16
11	M	M	Saint-Saëns—"Havanaise"
12	M	U	Menotti—The Shepherds' Chorus, from "Amahl and the Night Visitors"
13	M	U	Brubeck—"Blue Rondo a la Turk"
14	m	M	Brubeck—"Unsquare Dance"
15	m	U	Webber—The Temple, from "Jesus Christ Superstar"
16	M	M	Nigerian Folk Song—"Saturday Night"
17	M	M	Lalo—"Symphonie Espagnole," Op. 21
18	m	M	Dvorák—"Cello Concerto in B Minor," Op. 104
19	M	U	Bernstein—America, from "West Side Story"
20	M	U	Menotti—"The Unicorn"
21	M	M	Britten—There Is No Rose, from "A Ceremony of Carols"
22	M	M	Tschaikovsky—"Symphony No. 5"
23	m	M	Alfvén—"Midsommarvarka," Op. 19
24	M	U	Britten—In Freezing Winter Night, from "A Ceremony of Carols"
25	M	M	Ravel—"Rapsodie Espagnole"
26	M	U	Webber—Everything's All Right, from "Jesus Christ Superstar"
27	M	M	Gershwin—"Rhapsody in Blue"
28	m	U	Schifrin—Theme from "Mission Impossible"
29	m	M	Saint-Saëns—"Cello Concerto in A minor," Op. 33
30	M	U	Thomson—"Four Saints in Three Acts"

[35]

R1

R2

T1

T2

BIBLIOGRAPHY

Apel, Willi. *Harvard Dictionary of Music*, 2d ed. Cambridge: The Belknap Press of Harvard University Press, 1969.

Colwell, Richard. "The Development of the Music Achievement Test Series," *Council for Research in Music Education*, Bulletin No. 22 (Fall 1970):57–72.

———. *Music Achievement Tests*. Chicago: Follett, 1965.

Culver, Florence R. "A Study of the *Musical Aptitude Profile*." Master's thesis, University of Iowa, 1965.

Dittemore, Edgar. "An Investigation of Some Musical Capabilities of Elementary School Children." Ph.D. dissertation, University of Iowa, 1968.

Durost, Walter N., et al. *Metropolitan Achievement Tests*. New York: Harcourt Brace Jovanovich, 1970.

Fosha, R. Leon. "A Study of the Concurrent Validity of the *Musical Aptitude Profile*." Ph.D. dissertation, University of Iowa, 1964.

Gordon, Edwin. "Intercorrelations Among *Musical Aptitude Profile* and Seashore Measures of Musical Talents Subtests," *Journal of Research in Music Education*, 17 (1969):263–271.

———. *Iowa Tests of Music Literacy*. Iowa City: Bureau of Educational Research and Service, Division of Extension and University Services, University of Iowa, 1971.

———. *Musical Aptitude Profile Manual*. Boston: Houghton Mifflin, 1965.

———. *Psychology of Music Teaching*. Englewood Cliffs, N.J.: Prentice-Hall, 1971.

Harrington, Charles J. "An Investigation of the Primary Level *Musical Aptitude Profile* for Use with Second and Third Grade Students," *Journal of Research in Music Education* 17 (1969):359–368.

Hatfield, Warren G. "An Investigation of the Diagnostic Validity of the *Musical Aptitude Profile* with Respect to Instrumental Music Performance." Ph.D. dissertation, University of Iowa, 1967.

Lehman, Paul R. *Tests and Measurements in Music*. Englewood Cliffs, N.J.: Prentice-Hall, 1968.

Lindquist, E. F. *Design and Analysis of Experiments*. Boston: Houghton Mifflin, 1953.

Mohatt, James L. "A Study of the Validity of the *Iowa Tests of Music Literacy*." *Experimental Research in the Psychology of Music*:7. Studies in the Psychology of Music, vol. 7. Iowa City: University of Iowa Press, 1971.

Ottmann, Robert W. "A Statistical Investigation of the Influence of Selected Factors on the Skill of Sightsinging." Ph.D. dissertation, North Texas State University, 1956.

Schleuter, Stanley. "An Investigation of the Interrelation of Personality Traits, Musical Aptitude, and Musical Achievement." *Experimental Research in the Psychology of Music*:7. Studies in the Psychology of Music, vol. 8. Iowa City: University of Iowa Press, 1972.

Swinchoski, Albert A. "A Standardized Music Achievement Test Battery for the

Intermediate Grades," *Journal of Research in Music Education* 13 (1965): 159–168.

Swindell, Warren C. "An Investigation of the Adequacy of the Content and Difficulty Levels of the *Iowa Tests of Music Literacy*." Ph.D. dissertation, University of Iowa, 1970.

Thayer, Robert W. "An Investigation of the Interrelation of Personality Traits, Musical Achievement, and Different Measures of Musical Aptitude," *Experimental Research in the Psychology of Music:8*. Studies in the Psychology of Music, vol. 8. Iowa City: University of Iowa Press, 1972.

TOWARD THE DEVELOPMENT OF A TAXONOMY OF TONAL PATTERNS AND RHYTHM PATTERNS: EVIDENCE OF DIFFICULTY LEVEL AND GROWTH RATE

Edwin Gordon

Educational psychologists generally believe that fluent reading—reading with comprehension—is an outgrowth of viewing words through a semantic feature-analytic approach. That is, it is the words and the organization of words on a page, and not necessarily the recognition of alphabetic characteristics which constitute the words, that most efficiently generate meaning in the mind of the reader. Obviously, it is to the advantage of the reader to be able to group written matter into larger and larger units, such as letters into words, words into phrases, and phrases into sentences. In his recent book, *Understanding Reading*, Frank Smith elucidates this over-all concept:

> It is necessary at this point to clarify the relation between "learning the alphabet" and learning to read. There is an empirically well-founded correlation between the ability of children to identify letters and their ability to learn words, leading some theorists to believe that learning letters is a necessary first step for learning to identify words, and even that word identification must depend on letter-recognition skills. It is one of the basic aspects of my analysis of reading, of course, that the distinctive features of letters are the distinctive features of words, and also the distinctive features of meaning. Anything that will distinguish two letters is capable of distinguishing two words or two meanings. But that does not entail that learning the alphabet must precede learning words or comprehension. Quite the reverse; since the features of letters and words are the same, one might just as well learn what the features are from words as from letters. Certainly it will be easier to read if one learns [speaks] some words first (as most children do).[1]

There is a direct relationship between learning to read a spoken language and learning to read music. Specifically, principles regarding how we learn

Edwin Gordon is professor of music and education and Director of Music Education at the State University of New York at Buffalo.

[1] Frank Smith. *Understanding Reading* (New York: Holt. Rinehart and Winston, 1971). p. 227.

[39]

to read music are epitomized in *The Psychology of Music Teaching* in the following way:

> Understanding of music acquired through aural perception of tonality, kinesthetic feeling for meter, and sensitivity to musical expression is developed through singing and rhythmic activities. . . .
>
> In accordance with his basic musical aptitudes for developing tonal sense and rhythmic feeling, a person acquires [by rote] an oral vocabulary of tonal and rhythm patterns. The research of Bean,[2] Broman,[3] Mainwaring,[4] Ortmann,[5] Petzold,[6] and Van Nuys and Weaver[7] implies that the development of an oral vocabulary (by rote) of significant tonal and rhythm patterns constitutes the *experience* through which meaning is given to music, so that musical meaning can be associated with music notation for reading comprehension (just as a rote vocabulary of phrases of the spoken word constitutes the vehicle through which meaning is given to the written word). Like the relationship of the alphabet to language, the spelling of pitch names and the fractional values of notes are useful only as *theoretical* explanations of music notation after one has already acquired the fundamental ability of reading music through meaning. Because it takes more than one note to make a meaningful tonal or rhythm pattern, the knowledge of the pitch name or of the arithmetic value of one isolated note does not constitute readiness or ability to read music.[8]

It should be recognized that the terms "word" and "pattern" function synonymously in language reading and in music reading. Specifically, in the same manner that one learns to speak words by rote (and not necessarily memorize the names of letters of the alphabet) as a basis (readiness) for efficiently learning to read English, one learns to perform tonal and rhythm patterns by rote (and not necessarily memorize the pitch names or arithmetic values of individual notes) as a basis (readiness) for efficiently learning to read music. In this regard, the implication of the last sentence

---

2 Kenneth L. Bean, "An Experimental Approach to the Reading of Music," *Psychological Monographs* 50 (1938):80.

3 Keith La Vern Broman, "The Effects of Subjective Rhythmic Grouping Under the Influence of Variable Rates" (Ph.D. diss., University of Indiana, 1956).

4 James Mainwaring, "Kinesthetic Factors in the Recall of Musical Experience," *British Journal of Educational Psychology* 3 (1933):284–307.

5 Otto Ortmann, "Span of Vision in Note Reading," *Yearbook of the Music Educators National Conference* (1937):88–93.

6 Robert Petzold, *Auditory Perception of Musical Sounds by Children in the First Six Grades* (Madison: University of Wisconsin, 1966).

7 K. Van Nuys and H. E. Weaver, "Memory Span and Visual Pauses in Reading Rhythms and Melodies," *Psychological Monographs* 55 (1943):33–50.

8 Edwin Gordon, *The Psychology of Music Teaching* (Englewood Cliffs, N.J.: Prentice-Hall, 1971), p. 66.

in the quotation from Smith's text is of particular importance. In amplification, Smith states ". . . the fact that almost all children have acquired a good deal of verbal fluency before they face the task of learning to read has . . . significance for understanding the reading process."[9] Further, ". . . reading is not a matter of going from words to meaning, but rather from meaning to words."[10]

In general, there is, unfortunately, a lack of correspondence between pedagogical procedures and evidence which suggests how students most efficiently learn to read music. A crucial factor which would seem to contribute to this incongruity is that although music psychologists have been aware of the importance of the role of tonal and rhythm patterns in the development of music literacy ability, only recently have tonal and rhythm patterns been seminally organized according to their musical structure in *The Psychology of Music Teaching.* Moreover, the comparative over-all difficulty of patterns must still be determined before they can be most efficiently used in conjunction with proper pedagogical procedures. Therefore, this investigation represents the initial phase of the development of a taxonomy of tonal and rhythm patterns and the objective determination of the difficulty level and growth rate of these patterns. It is anticipated that the findings of this investigation will aid music educators in developing systematic procedures for teaching music literacy. That is, knowledge of the difficulty level and growth rate, in addition to the musical organization, of tonal and rhythm patterns should serve to identify specific content and establish sequence for a course of study through which students learn to perceive and ultimately read and write music. Such a course of study, in which patterns could define criterion-referenced skills, would necessarily embody pedagogical procedures for teaching to students' individual musical differences. And it should not go unmentioned that the results of this investigation may contribute to more adequate control of future experimental research in the psychology of music.

DESIGN OF THE INVESTIGATION

A unique opportunity was advantageously pursued to gather the data to conduct this study. The test results of 18,680 public school students who participated in the 1971 national standardization program of the six Levels of the *Iowa Tests of Music Literacy (ITML)* were available to the writer.

---

9 Smith, p. 45.
10 Smith. p. 35.

These students, enrolled in grades 4 through 12, represented 27 school systems in 13 of the United States. In the standardization process, norms were developed for three grade ranges: elementary school—grades 4 through 6; junior high school—grades 7 through 9; and senior high school—grades 10 through 12. Specifically, there are elementary grade range norms for *ITML* Levels 1, 2, and 3; and junior high school and senior high school range norms for *ITML* Levels 1, 2, 3, 4, 5, and 6. A detailed description of the standardization program may be found in the *ITML Manual*.[11]

Each of the six Levels of the *Iowa Tests of Music Literacy* comprises six parallel subtests (which become more complex from Level to Level) that are classified into two divisions: *Tonal Concepts* and *Rhythmic Concepts*. Three subtests are included in each of the two divisions. They are titled Tonal *Aural Perception, Reading Recognition,* and *Notational Understanding;* and Rhythmic *Aural Perception, Reading Recognition,* and *Notational Understanding.* For the *Aural Perception* and *Reading Recognition* subtests in each division, the student simply indicates his response to each item by filling one of two ovals on the answer sheet, or he may choose the "in doubt" option. However, in the Tonal *Notational Understanding* subtests the student hears from six to eight nine-tone patterns (depending on the *ITML* Level) on a tape recording, but only four interspersed tones are indicated for each pattern on the answer sheet. The student writes, by filling one of two given ovals which are note heads on a staff on the answer sheet, the pitch of each of the remaining five tones in the pattern. Similarly, in the Rhythmic *Notational Understanding* subtests the student hears from nine to fourteen rhythm patterns of various lengths (depending on the *ITML* Level) on a tape recording, which are only partially written on the answer sheet. The student completes the rhythmic notation of each rhythm pattern by filling appropriate ovals which are note heads, flags, beams, ties, and/or rests on the answer sheet.

The individual test items in all six Levels of the *ITML* battery include tonal or rhythmic patterns as musically organized in *The Psychology of Music Teaching*.[12] In the *Tonal Concepts* divisions, depending on the specific *ITML* Level and subtest, the test items (which include two or more tonal patterns) are in dorian, phrygian, lydian, mixolydian, or locrian tonality, and some are nontonal.[13] In the *Rhythmic Concepts* divisions, depending on the specific *ITML* Level and subtest, the test items (which

---

11 Edwin Gordon, *Iowa Tests of Music Literacy Manual* (Iowa City: University of Iowa, 1970), pp. 95–97.

12 Gordon, *The Psychology of Music Teaching*, pp. 69–72.

13 For a detailed explanation of these terms, see pages 96–98 in *The Psychology of Music Teaching* and pages 9 and 10 in the *ITML Manual.*

include two or more rhythm patterns) are in either duple, triple, or mixed or unusual meter.[14]

Because of the intended purposes of *ITML*, unison major and minor tonal patterns and duple and triple rhythm patterns are emphasized in the test items of the battery. As a result, there are relatively few test items in the less familiar modes, and even fewer two-part, chordal, and nontonal test items. Similarly, there are relatively few test items in mixed and unusual meter. Therefore, because there were not enough items in the *ITML* battery (1) in tonalities other than major and minor or (2) in meters other than duple and triple, from which viable interpretations could be drawn, the characteristics of only major and minor tonal patterns (in the tonal test items) and duple and triple rhythm patterns (in the rhythm test items) were studied in this investigation.

Test items which include major and minor tonal patterns and test items which include duple and triple rhythm patterns are found in Levels 1, 2, 3, and 4 of the *ITML* battery. Thus, only the test results from the standardization program for *ITML* Levels 1, 2, and 3 for students in all three grade ranges and for *ITML* Level 4 for students in just the upper two grade ranges could be analyzed for purposes of this investigation. From the total number of students who were administered *ITML* in the standardization program, the results of a random sample of 250 students in each of the previously described eleven norms groups were selected for analysis, resulting in a grand total of 2,750.

The initial step in the investigation was the derivation of the difficulty and discrimination levels of the test items in the *ITML* battery. The results of the item analyses for all subjects, including those of *ITML* Levels 5 and 6 to facilitate any further comparisons which the reader may wish to make, can be found in Appendix A. (For ease in reading, decimals which usually precede correlation coefficients and percentages have been deleted.)

The discrimination headings in Appendix A refer to point biserial correlation coefficients between items (2 was assigned for a correct answer and 1 for an incorrect answer) and respective Tonal and Rhythmic *Aural Perception* and *Reading Recognition* subtest scores. Because of the unique nature of scoring the Tonal and Rhythmic *Notational Understanding* subtests (credit is given for partially correct answers in terms of continuous points for an entire item and therefore, of course, the items are not scored dichotomously),[15] discrimination values represent Pearson product-moment coeffi-

---

[14] For a detailed explanation of these terms, see pages 69–72 in *The Psychology of Music Teaching* and pages 10 and 11 in the *ITML Manual*.

[15] For a detailed explanation of the scoring procedure for these subtests, refer to pages 73–75 in the *ITML Manual*.

cients between the sum of students' correct responses on a complete test item and their corresponding subtest score. Also, it should be mentioned that in computing difficulty levels for the Tonal and Rhythmic *Notational Understanding* subtests, using the standard formula, continuous scores for the individual items were substituted for the number of students who answered an item correctly in the higher and lower scoring groups.

The next step in the investigation was the systematic extensive documentation of a Musical Organization Taxonomy of Tonal and Rhythm Patterns which follows the system set forth in *The Psychology of Music Teaching*[16] and the *ITML Manual*.[17] (As previously indicated, for the purpose of this investigation, only major and minor tonal patterns and duple and triple rhythm patterns were considered.)

Concerning tonal functions, groupings of at least two, more frequently three, and no more than five tones were identified as tonal patterns. Similarly, series which included at least two but no more than six notes, sometimes combined with rests, were identified as rhythm patterns. Then the patterns were musically organized into divisions[18] of Basic (simpler patterns) and Complex (more complicated patterns) in the following manner.

Musical Organization Taxonomy

BASIC MAJOR TONAL PATTERNS
    Tonic Function
    Dominant Function
    Subdominant Function

BASIC DUPLE RHYTHM PATTERNS
    Tempo and Meter Beats
    Fractionations and Elongations
    Upbeats

COMPLEX MAJOR TONAL PATTERNS
    Chromaticism
    Combined Harmonic Functions
    Expanded Harmonic Functions

COMPLEX DUPLE RHYTHM PATTERNS
    Fractionations and Elongations
    Rests
    Ties
    Upbeats

---

16 Gordon, *The Psychology of Music Teaching*, pp. 69–72, 96–98.

17 Gordon, *ITML Manual*, pp. 9–11.

18 The titles of the divisions and subparts differ somewhat from those offered in *The Psychology of Music Teaching* and the *Iowa Tests of Music Literacy Manual*. Specifically, divisions referred to as Uncommon are here called Complex. The reason for this change is to obviate any confusion which might arise from the fact that Complex Patterns are not found any less frequently in music (that is, they are not any more uncommon) than are the Basic Patterns. And, the present titles of the subparts should contribute to making the nature of their musical structure more clear.

BASIC MINOR TONAL PATTERNS	BASIC TRIPLE RHYTHM PATTERNS
Tonic Function	Tempo and Meter Beats
Dominant Function	Fractionations and Elongations
Subdominant Function	Upbeats

COMPLEX MINOR TONAL PATTERNS	COMPLEX TRIPLE RHYTHM PATTERNS
Chromaticism	Fractionations and Elongations
Combined Harmonic Functions	Rests
Expanded Harmonic Functions	Ties
	Upbeats

The tonal division and subpart titles in the Musical Organization Taxonomy should be self-explanatory with the possible exceptions of Combined Harmonic Functions and Expanded Harmonic Functions. The former incorporates patterns which suggest more than one implied harmonic function (for example, both tonic and dominant) and the latter incorporates patterns which suggest implied harmonic functions other than tonic, dominant, or subdominant (that is supertonic, mediant, submediant, or leading tone). Of course, an isolated tonal pattern cannot be considered either major or minor (even though given theoretical names, based on intervallic structure of the pattern, unfortunately might duplicate a description of tonality) until it becomes an integral part of an intact melody. In a musical (not theoretical) context, a tonal pattern is major if the interaction of all patterns in the melody in which it is comprised suggests a resting tone (tonic) of "Do," and as minor if the interaction of all patterns in the melody suggests a resting tone (tonic) of "La."[19]

Regarding the rhythmic division and subpart titles in the Musical Organization Taxonomy, they are uniquely defined and explained in *The Psychology of Music Teaching*. However, a discussion of some of the subpart titles (namely, Tempo and Meter Beats, and Fractionations and Elongations) should provide for immediate clarification. As an introduction to these concepts in *The Psychology of Music Teaching*, a definition of rhythm is given:

> Rhythm is comprised of three basic elements. They are 1) tempo beats, 2) meter beats, and 3) melodic rhythm. In music these elements interact in a composite polyrhythmic manner and give rise to what is referred to as rhythm.[20]

---

[19] The concept of "tonality" follows the definition given by Willi Apel in the *Harvard Dictionary of Music*. "In the broadest sense of the word, loyalty to a tonic." See 2d. ed. (Cambridge: Harvard University Press, 1969), p. 855.
[20] Gordon, *The Psychology of Music Teaching*, p. 67.

Tempo beats are explained as follows:

> Of the three basic elements of rhythm, tempo beats are fundamental be-
> cause they provide the foundation upon which all other elements of rhythm
> are superimposed. . . . Notational examples of tempo beats [as they function
> in duple and triple meter, respectively] are given below.[21]

Concerning meter beats:

> Meter—in music, poetry, and speech—'moves' in two's and three's.[22] Duple
> meter is derived by superimposing two equally spaced beats within the dur-
> ation of a tempo beat. Triple meter is derived by superimposing three equally
> spaced beats within the duration of a tempo beat. Notational examples of
> duple and triple meter beats, respectively, are given below.[23]

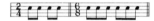

Finally, fractionations and elongations are explained through their relationship to melodic rhythm.

> Melodic rhythm comprises rhythm patterns that correspond to the rhythm
> of the melody or to the rhythm of the text . . . these patterns are superim-
> posed on meter beats and tempo beats. However, melodic rhythm patterns
> can be coincidental with meter beats and tempo beats, and they also include
> fractionations and elongations of meter beats and elongations of tempo
> beats.[24]

21 Gordon, *The Psychology of Music Teaching*, p. 67.

22 In regard to meter, it is instructive to note Le Cerf de La Viéville's statement in
Bourdelot-Bonnet's *Histoire de la Musique*, vol. I (Paris, 1725), p. 307, ". . . so there
are in general only two measures, that in two-time, and that in three; in vain would you
wish to imagine others." And Charles Masson in *Nouveau Traité*, Second Edition (Paris,
1701), p. 6, declares that: "Although there appear to be a quantity of different measures,
I believe that it is useful to point out that there is only the number two or three which
divides them . . . ." Both of these quotes may be found in Robert Donington, *The Interpretation of Early Music* (London: Faber and Faber, 1963), p. 346.

23 Gordon, *The Psychology of Music Teaching*, p. 68.

24 Gordon, *The Psychology of Music Teaching*, p. 68.

Patterns within Complex Fractionations and Elongations subparts in the Musical Organization Taxonomy differ from those within Basic Fractionations and Elongations subparts in that for the former, some notes in a pattern are durationally longer than one tempo and/or meter beat or because some notes are durationally shorter than half of a meter beat. And, Complex Upbeat patterns differ from Basic Upbeat patterns in that the former always begin on a tempo beat or because they may include ties.

Although the division titles for the Musical Organization Taxonomy of Rhythm Patterns should be implicitly understood by virtue of the above clarification of the subpart titles, a final quotation from the *ITML Manual* should serve to solidify the concepts of duple and triple meter:

> The terms 'duple' and 'triple', like those of 'mixed' and 'unusual', are referred to as types of meter. Patterns written in duple meter are those which generally have a 2 or 4 as the upper numeral of the meter signature. Patterns written in triple meter are those which generally have a 3, 6, or 12 as the upper numeral of the meter signature.[25]

The Musical Organization Taxonomy of Tonal Patterns is presented in notational form, including divisions and subparts, in Table 1. The Musical Organization Taxonomy of Rhythm Patterns is similarly presented in Table 2. It should be explained that when dyads are notated between single tones in some tonal patterns, this indicates that one or the other of the tones in the dyad in conjunction with the two single tones represents a pattern. Also, it should be stressed that the vertical lines which separate the patterns, especially in regard to the rhythm patterns, are not meant to indicate measure lines.

The last step in gathering the data for the investigation was the musical analysis of each test item in every *ITML* subtest so that inherent patterns which correspond to the tonal patterns in Table 1 and to the rhythm patterns in Table 2 could be identified. First, items in the *ITML* tonal subtests were identified as being either in major or minor tonality if the tonic was "Do" or "La," respectively. Then the tonal patterns were extracted—the key, register, and clef in which the item was written notwithstanding. In some cases tonal patterns were contiguous in the test items (for example, the final tone of one pattern became the beginning tone of another pattern). Finally, the rhythm patterns were extracted from the test items. Only test items with a meter signature of 2/4 (duple) and 6/8 (triple) were examined. It might be mentioned that although test items in duple and triple meter are also written with meter signatures other than 2/4 and 6/8, re-

---

25 Gordon, *ITML Manual,* p. 10.

Table 1

Musical Organization
Taxonomy of Tonal Patterns
Basic Major Tonal Patterns

[48]

Complex Major Tonal Patterns

Basic Minor Tonal Patterns

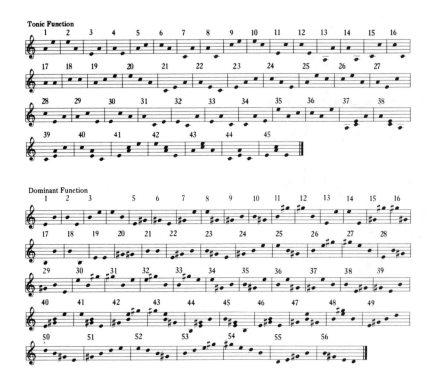

Complex Minor Tonal Patterns

Table 2

Musical Organization
Taxonomy of Rhythm Patterns

Basic Duple Rhythm Patterns

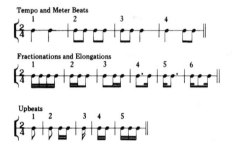

Complex Duple Rhythm Patterns

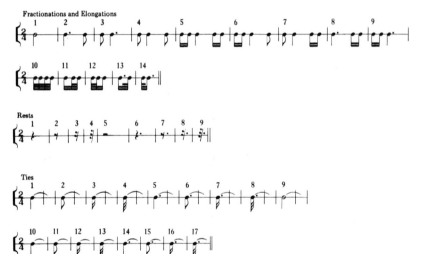

Basic Triple Rhythm Patterns

Complex Triple Rhythm Patterns

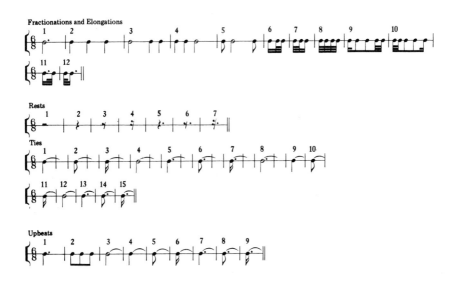

[53]

spectively, in the Rhythmic *Reading Recognition* and *Notational Understanding* subtests, only the meter signatures 2/4 and 6/8 are employed in the Rhythmic *Aural Perception* subtests.

The patterns in the items in the Tonal and Rhythmic *Aural Perception* and *Notational Understanding* subtests were relatively easy to identify. However, in the Tonal and Rhythmic *Reading Recognition* subtests, the student is to indicate whether or not the series of notes on the answer sheet is in fact that heard on the tape recording. The notes in the test items on the answer sheet in these subtests are therefore not always those performed on the tape recording. As a result the problem arose as to whether to consider the notated test item or the performed test item, when they are not the same, for extracting patterns. The decision was made to identify patterns separately in test items notated on the answer sheet and those performed on the tape recording for both Tonal and Rhythmic *Reading Recognition* subtests.

The possibility should be recognized that some tonal and rhythm patterns might have been fortuitously overlooked (though probably not consistently) in the examination of the *ITML* test items. Also, it should be remembered that there are tonal and rhythm patterns which are inherent in the *ITML* test items but are not represented in the Musical Organization Taxonomy of Tonal and Rhythm Patterns found in Tables 1 and 2.

RESULTS OF THE INVESTIGATION

The relevant tonal and rhythm patterns were initially documented so that it could be determined from which *ITML* test items they were extracted. This arduous task was undertaken because given patterns are found in different contexts in various *ITML* test items which do not usually share exact difficulty levels and growth rates. The context of an *ITML* test item, as well as a given pattern itself, could, of course, affect these indexes. Therefore, it was assumed that the reader would want to determine for himself the extent to which factors such as key signature, clef, register, ledger lines, flagged and beamed notation, and most importantly, the presence, order, and sequence of other patterns in an *ITML* test item might have influenced the difficulty level and growth rate of a given pattern. Thus, each tonal pattern found in the *ITML* battery is notated in Appendix B adjacent to all *ITML* test items in which it was comprised and similarly, each rhythm pattern is presented with corresponding *ITML* test items in Appendix C.

The sequence of the presentation of the patterns in Appendixes B and C is similar to that found in the Musical Organization Taxonomy of Tonal Patterns and Rhythm Patterns in Tables 1 and 2, respectively. In Appen-

[54]

dixes B and C, it will be noticed that the patterns are numbered in the first column and notated in the second column. The numerals correspond to the numerical sequence of the Tonal and the Rhythm patterns in the Musical Organization Taxonomy in Tables 1 and 2. Therefore, when a numeral is skipped between patterns in Appendixes B and C, this indicates that the pattern associated with that numeral in the Musical Organization Taxonomy was not found in any *ITML* test item. In the third column, the *ITML* Level and subtest to which the test item belongs is indicated. The *ITML* Levels are simply numbered 1 through 4. For the subtests, the numerals 1 through 3 are used; 1 indicates the *Aural Perception* subtest, 2 the *Reading Recognition* subtest, and 3 the *Notational Understanding* subtest. The letters T and B are employed to further identify the *Reading Recognition* subtest items. The T indicates that the pattern is heard in the *ITML* test item on the tape recording, the B indicates that the pattern in the *ITML* test item is seen on the answer sheet (booklet), and T–B indicates that the same pattern is heard in the *ITML* test item on the tape recording and that it is also seen on the answer sheet. The *ITML* test item is notated in the fourth column (when more than one test item is reproduced for a pattern for a given subtest it is, of course, because the pattern is found in all of the *ITML* test items shown). In the fifth column, the difficulty level of the *ITML* test items for students in grades 4 through 6 is reported. Similarly, the difficulty levels of the *ITML* test item for students in grades 7 through 9 and grades 10 through 12 are reported in columns six and seven, respectively. (These difficulty levels are reproduced from Appendix A.) The composite difficulty level (the average for the three grade ranges) of the *ITML* test item is shown in the eighth column and the growth rate is described in the ninth column. The growth rate is represented by the difference between the difficulty level of the *ITML* test item for students in grades 4 through 6 and for students in grades 10 through 12. The tenth and eleventh columns are included for the purpose of reporting the over-all difficulty level and growth rate for a given pattern when it is found in more than one *ITML* test item. Specifically, these over-all data were derived by averaging the composite difficulty levels of each *ITML* test item in which a given pattern was found and similarly by averaging the composite growth rates of that same collection of *ITML* test items. (Of course, when a pattern was found in only one test item in an *ITML* subtest, the over-all difficulty levels and growth rates reported in the tenth and eleventh columns are the same as the composites found in the eighth and ninth columns, respectively.) In the final two columns, the difficulty level and growth rates for each pattern are categorized verbally (not numerically). The definitions of the verbal categorization abbreviations are:

Difficulty Level	Growth Rate
VE—Very Easy	VL—Very Low
E—Easy	L—Low
M—Moderate	T—Typical
D—Difficult	H—High
VD—Very Difficult	VH—Very High

The verbal categorizations for the patterns were derived in the following manner. First, the over-all difficulty levels (taken from the tenth column in Appendixes B and C) and the over-all growth rates (taken from the eleventh column in Appendixes B and C) of the patterns within each Musical Organization Taxonomy subpart were averaged for all Levels combined of each *ITML* subtest. After the means were calculated, standard deviations for each of these collections of difficulty levels and growth rates were computed. Then, for all Levels combined of each *ITML* subtest, if the mean difficulty level for a pattern comprised in a given subpart of the Musical Organization Taxonomy fell within one standard deviation above or below the mean for all patterns included in that Musical Organization Taxonomy subpart, the pattern was categorized as being of Moderate difficulty. Patterns with difficulty levels between one and two, and two and three standard deviations below the mean were categorized as Difficult and Very Difficult, respectively. In the same manner, patterns with difficulty levels between one and two, and two and three standard deviations above the mean were categorized as Easy and Very Easy, respectively. The same procedures were used for verbally categorizing the patterns in terms of growth rate. Specifically, for all Levels combined of each *ITML* subtest, if the mean growth rate for a pattern comprised in a given Musical Organization Taxonomy subpart fell within one standard deviation above or below the mean for all patterns included in that Musical Organization Taxonomy subpart, the pattern was categorized as having Typical growth. Patterns with growth rates between one and two, and two and three standard deviations below the mean were categorized as having Low and Very Low growth, respectively; those between one and two, and two and three standard deviations above the mean were categorized as having High and Very High growth, respectively. The mean, standard deviation, and number (N) of all patterns comprised in each Tonal and Rhythm Musical Organization Taxonomy subpart, for all Levels combined of each *ITML* subtest, are presented in Tables 3 through 8. In these same tables may also be found the verbal categorizations for each complete Tonal and Rhythm Musical Organization Taxonomy subpart for all Levels combined of each *ITML* subtest. The procedures used for deriving the verbal categorizations for the complete subparts were identical to those employed for categorizing the indi-

[56]

vidual patterns. However, for the former comparisons, the over-all means (found at the bottom of Tables 3 through 8) for the Musical Organization Taxonomy subparts were averaged and standard deviations were computed. Corresponding data and verbal categorizations for all patterns which comprise each *ITML Tonal Concepts* and *Rhythmic Concepts* subtest, respectively, all Levels combined, are presented in Tables 9 and 10, which are organized in the same way as Tables 3 through 8.

The manner of presentation of the patterns in Appendix D (which includes the tonal patterns) and Appendix E (which includes the rhythm patterns) is different from that of Appendixes B and C in that the patterns are grouped according to Difficulty Level Taxonomy and Growth Rate Taxonomy within, all Levels combined, each *ITML* subtest. The numerical order of the patterns is, however, kept intact. The Growth Rate Taxonomies immediately follow the Difficulty Level Taxonomies within each Musical Organization Taxonomy subpart.

Table 3

Difficulty and Growth Comparisons for Taxonomic Tonal
Patterns Comprised in the *ITML* Aural Perception Subtests

	DIFFICULTY				GROWTH			
	Mean	SD	N	Category	Mean	SD	N	Category
BASIC MAJOR TONAL PATTERNS								
Tonic Function	64.7	4.59	20	M	21.4	2.45	20	T
Dominant Function	61.1	4.43	14	M	25.4	9.42	14	H
Subdominant Function	57.6	8.11	10	M	22.0	6.43	10	T
COMPLEX MAJOR TONAL PATTERNS								
Chromaticism	54.0	3.22	6	D	16.4	6.21	5	L
Combined								
Harmonic Functions	71.2	10.40	28	VE	16.4	5.56	28	L
Expanded								
Harmonic Functions	67.8	6.96	6	E	21.0	5.26	6	T
BASIC MINOR TONAL PATTERNS								
Tonic Function	57.0	5.99	23	M	18.2	6.14	23	T
Dominant Function	53.9	6.17	9	D	16.2	5.77	9	L
Subdominant Function	53.1	2.46	9	D	16.2	4.39	9	L
COMPLEX MINOR TONAL PATTERNS								
Chromaticism	57.7	4.92	3	M	21.3	1.88	3	T
Combined								
Harmonic Functions	61.0	7.53	24	M	17.3	5.60	24	T
Expanded								
Harmonic Functions	60.0	9.97	4	M	25.8	2.68	4	H
OVER-ALL	59.9	5.41	12		19.8	3.37	12	

The patterns in Appendixes D and E are not numbered because although they are presented in the same numerical order as in the Musical Organization Taxonomy of Tonal Patterns and Rhythm Patterns in Tables 1 and 2, the order is reestablished beginning with each of the five Difficulty Level and Growth Rate Taxonomies within each Musical Organization Taxonomy subpart for each *ITML* subtest. (The lack of continuity in pattern numbers proved to be distracting.) Therefore, comparisons of Tables 1 and 2 with Appendixes D and E, respectively, are best accomplished by identifying patterns through musical notation rather than by numerals. Also, it will be noticed in Appendixes D and E that the patterns within some Musical Organization Taxonomy subparts are not identical for each *ITML* subtest because, of course, the same patterns would not be expected to be found in every *ITML* subtest. Further, not all of the tonal and rhythm patterns given in the Musical Organization Taxonomies in Tables 1 and 2 are ac-

Table 4

Difficulty and Growth Comparisons for Taxonomic Tonal
Patterns Comprised in the *ITML* Reading Recognition Subtests

	DIFFICULTY				GROWTH			
	Mean	SD	N	Category	Mean	SD	N	Category
BASIC MAJOR TONAL PATTERNS								
Tonic Function	74.5	12.02	23	M	15.4	5.50	23	L
Dominant Function	78.8	10.96	14	M	19.5	13.49	14	T
Subdominant Function	80.4	6.94	10	E	19.4	4.34	10	T
COMPLEX MAJOR TONAL PATTERNS								
Chromaticism	76.6	14.99	5	M	18.0	13.71	5	T
Combined								
Harmonic Functions	82.4	2.09	27	E	16.7	7.85	27	L
Expanded								
Harmonic Functions	71.3	14.52	7	D	23.4	9.09	7	T
BASIC MINOR TONAL PATTERNS								
Tonic Function	75.8	7.94	20	M	23.1	4.47	20	T
Dominant Function	75.3	8.26	12	M	22.8	7.98	12	T
Subdominant Function	78.5	8.61	11	M	22.1	5.46	11	T
COMPLEX MINOR TONAL PATTERNS								
Chromaticism	72.8	12.88	4	D	25.8	5.06	4	H
Combined								
Harmonic Functions	75.5	13.56	27	M	20.2	7.24	27	T
Expanded								
Harmonic Functions	77.5	6.97	6	M	26.0	5.90	6	H
OVER-ALL	76.6	2.99	12		21.0	3.25	12	

counted for in Appendixes D and E because the *ITML* test items do not include all patterns in the Musical Organization Taxonomy.

Finally, it should be understood that some Difficulty Level and Growth Rate categories might not appear in Appendixes D and E because in the statistical analysis, patterns were not always found in all five Difficulty Level and Growth Rate categories within each Musical Organization Taxonomy subpart, particularly for every *ITML* subtest.

IMPLICATIONS OF THE INVESTIGATIONS

The conclusion that music literacy skill contributes positively to over-all musical development is ineluctable. Palisca, below, stresses this concept as

Table 5

Difficulty and Growth Comparisons for Taxonomic Tonal
Patterns Comprised in the *ITML* Notational Understanding Subtests

	DIFFICULTY				GROWTH			
	Mean	SD	N	Category	Mean	SD	N	Category
BASIC MAJOR TONAL PATTERNS								
Tonic Function	65.3	12.33	22	M	20.0	8.48	22	T
Dominant Function	60.3	19.36	2	D	32.7	11.09	2	VH
Subdominant Function	67.7	11.84	3	M	28.7	6.94	3	H
COMPLEX MAJOR TONAL PATTERNS								
Chromaticism	75.3	0.48	3	M	19.0	4.24	3	T
Combined								
Harmonic Functions	75.1	7.84	21	M	23.3	8.72	21	T
Expanded								
Harmonic Functions	66.3	20.59	4	M	25.5	12.46	4	T
BASIC MINOR TONAL PATTERNS								
Tonic Function	67.9	8.26	14	M	17.5	4.44	14	T
Dominant Function	78.3	7.85	4	E	17.5	2.18	4	T
Subdominant Function	68.5	8.50	2	M	21.0	8.00	2	T
COMPLEX MINOR TONAL PATTERNS								
Chromaticism	68.5	5.68	4	M	17.0	1.22	4	T
Combined								
Harmonic Functions	66.3	20.59	4	M	18.5	5.15	19	T
Expanded								
Harmonic Functions	......	....	....	....°	......	....	....	....°
OVER-ALL	69.9	5.22	11		21.9	4.90	11	

° No patterns were found for this subpart.

[59]

well as the importance of the role of readiness (aural perception) for music literacy achievement. At the same time he gives credence to the fact that students best learn to read and write music when they are taught according to their individual differences in musical aptitude.

The development of musicality is the primary aim of music education from kindergarten through the 12th grade. Musicality is a quality universally understood by musicians, but a difficult one to define. The analogous quality with respect to language is verbal ability. Essentially, musicality is the capacity to express a musical idea accurately through pitch and time. Conversely, it is the capacity to grasp in its completeness and detail a musical statement heard. It can be assumed that a degree of musicality is a nat-

Table 6

Difficulty and Growth Comparisons for Taxonomic Rhythm
Patterns Comprised in the *ITML* Aural Perception Subtests

	DIFFICULTY				GROWTH			
	Mean	SD	N	Category	Mean	SD	N	Category
BASIC DUPLE RHYTHM PATTERNS								
Tempo and Meter Beats	61.3	3.90	3	M	13.3	3.77	3	T
Fractionations and								
Elongations	62.7	4.74	6	M	12.5	7.50	6	T
Upbeats	60.3	12.20	4	M	17.3	6.49	4	T
COMPLEX DUPLE RHYTHM PATTERNS								
Fractionations and								
Elongations	59.0	10.29	8	M	22.9	7.31	8	VH
Rests	......	....	....	....*	......	....	....	....*
Ties	67.2	7.14	3	E	15.3	10.04	3	T
Upbeats	59.7	8.72	3	M	12.3	7.84	3	T
BASIC TRIPLE RHYTHM PATTERNS								
Tempo and Meter Beats	60.8	2.86	4	M	12.0	5.70	4	T
Fractionations and								
Elongations	64.3	6.63	10	E	13.0	6.30	10	T
Upbeats	58.3	2.49	3	M	15.0	2.82	3	T
COMPLEX TRIPLE RHYTHM PATTERNS								
Fractionations and								
Elongations	59.7	8.65	3	M	9.0	2.16	3	L
Rests	......	....	....	....*	......	....	....	....*
Ties	50.3	0.94	3	D	20.0	3.56	3	H
Upbeats	54.7	3.30	3	D	17.3	5.44	3	T
OVER-ALL	59.9	4.30	12		15.0	3.69	12	

* No patterns were found for this subpart.

ural attribute of everyone. For each pupil there is a way in which his particular share of it can be tapped and developed.

Since in most people this ability is only approximate, its cultivation must be a continuous effort throughout a person's music education. A basic musicality should be developed, however, before the teaching of reading, notation, composing, or analysis is attempted, for these skills become mechanical and meaningless without it. As the teaching of reading and writing music progresses, corresponding progress should be expected in the ability to express and grasp musical ideas. With the growth of this capacity, greater attention can be given to the nature of the musical ideas themselves.[26]

Table 7

Difficulty and Growth Comparisons for Taxonomic Rhythm
Patterns Comprised in the *ITML* Reading Recognition Subtests

	DIFFICULTY				GROWTH			
	Mean	SD	N	Category	Mean	SD	N	Category
BASIC DUPLE RHYTHM PATTERNS								
Tempo and Meter Beats	67.7	4.08	3	M	17.3	0.94	3	L
Fractionations and								
Elongations	62.3	9.16	6	D	23.2	3.53	6	T
Upbeats	64.3	3.69	3	M	22.3	1.24	33	T
COMPLEX DUPLE RHYTHM PATTERNS								
Fractionations and								
Elongations	66.2	7.05	9	M	23.7	8.00	9	T
Rests	64.5	6.84	6	M	18.3	5.58	6	L
Ties	64.0	4.06	4	M	25.0	4.58	4	H
Upbeats	67.0	7.00	2	M	19.0	6.00	2	L
BASIC TRIPLE RHYTHM PATTERNS								
Tempo and Meter Beats	69.3	8.23	4	E	23.3	5.40	4	T
Fractionations and								
Elongations	64.4	5.72	12	M	24.8	8.67	13	H
Upbeats	67.0	3.00	2	M	20.5	2.34	2	T
COMPLEX TRIPLE RHYTHM PATTERNS								
Fractionations and								
Elongations	63.0	7.90	4	D	17.8	6.87	4	L
Rests	68.0	1.41	5	M	19.6	7.19	5	T
Ties	65.2	8.03	6	M	25.0	5.22	6	H
Upbeats	75.0	13.0	2	VE	23.0	1.00	2	T
OVER-ALL	66.3	3.10	14		21.6	2.65	14	

---

[26] Claude Palisca, ed., *Music in Our Schools*, Report of the Yale Seminar on Music Education (Washington. D.C.: Office of Education. 1964), p. 6.

[61]

As indicated in the beginning section of this paper, the mind grasps tonal patterns and rhythm patterns when we perceive, read, and write music. The patterns which are identified, organized, and categorized in this investigation can be used for helping students sequentially learn to become musically literate, particularly when pedagogical procedures are adapted to their individual musical differences. Before an explanation is undertaken of how this may be accomplished, a word of caution should be reiterated. Specifically, the results of this investigation should not be misconstrued as being representative of those which might have been derived from experimental research. Because the *Iowa Tests of Music Literacy* are designed to efficiently measure students' achievement, the quantity and

Table 8

Difficulty and Growth Comparisons for Taxonomic Rhythm
Patterns Comprised in the *ITML* Notational Understanding Subtests

	DIFFICULTY				GROWTH			
	Mean	SD	N	Category	Mean	SD	N	Category
BASIC DUPLE RHYTHM PATTERNS								
Tempo and Meter Beats	59.0	5.00	2	M	11.0	1.00	2	T
Fractionations and								
Elongations	58.5	0.87	4	M	10.0	3.46	4	T
Upbeats	39.0	7.00	2	D	7.5	2.50	2	L
COMPLEX DUPLE RHYTHM PATTERNS								
Fractionations and								
Elongations	56.3	6.72	4	M	13.5	4.98	4	T
Rests	60.0	4.00	2	M	16.0	1.41	2	H
Ties	51.0	8.00	2	M	6.5	0.50	2	L
Upbeats	......	....	....	....°	......	....	....	....°
BASIC TRIPLE RHYTHM PATTERNS								
Tempo and Meter Beats	72.7	7.40	3	E	19.3	0.94	3	H
Fractionations and								
Elongations	49.2	10.49	6	M	6.3	3.45	6	L
Upbeats	55.5	9.58	2	M	5.0	1.41	2	L
COMPLEX TRIPLE RHYTHM PATTERNS								
Fractionations and								
Elongations	......	....	....	....°	......	....	....	....°
Rests	62.0	4.00	2	M	13.0	4.00	2	T
Ties	63.0	....	1	M	14.0	....	1	T
Upbeats	......	....	....	....°	......	....	....	....°
OVER-ALL	56.9	9.53	11		11.1	4.24	11	

° No patterns were found for this subpart.

the nature of the presentation of the content in the battery is not best suited for forming the basis of an experimental study directed toward the identification, organization, and categorization of all possible tonal and rhythm patterns. Therefore, the results of this investigation should be considered inchoate. But nonetheless, when the implications are viewed with wisdom, they can serve well in developing at least an appropriate initial course of study in music literacy. As a consequence of this investigation, however, the design and procedures for analyzing data of an extensive experimental study (which should provide more inclusive information about typical tonal and rhythm patterns and those in less familiar modes and meters, and nontonal patterns) have been established, and it is planned that such a study will be originated in the near future.

To provide for the practical utilization (as opposed to the theoretical study) of the results of this investigation, the data in Appendixes D and E are collated in Tables 11 through 14 (tonal patterns) and Tables 15 through 18 (rhythm patterns). That is, in each table the Difficulty Level (on the upper line) and the Growth Rate (on the lower line) are reported together

Table 9

Difficulty and Growth Comparisons for Taxonomic Tonal Patterns
Comprised in the *ITML* Aural Perception, Reading Recognition,
and Notational Understanding Subtests

	DIFFICULTY				GROWTH			
	Mean	SD	N	Category	Mean	SD	N	Category
Aural Perception	59.9	5.41	12	D	19.8	3.37	12	L
Reading Recognition	76.6	2.99	12	E	21.0	3.25	12	T
Notational Understanding	69.9	5.22	11	M	21.9	4.90	11	H
OVER-ALL	68.8	6.86	3		20.9	0.86	3	

Table 10

Difficulty and Growth Comparisons for Taxonomic Rhythm Patterns
Comprised in the *ITML* Aural Perception, Reading Recognition,
and Notational Understanding Subtests

	DIFFICULTY				GROWTH			
	Mean	SD	N	Category	Mean	SD	N	Category
Aural Perception	59.9	4.30	12	M	15.0	3.69	12	T
Reading Recognition	66.3	3.10	14	E	21.6	2.65	14	H
Notational Understanding	56.9	9.53	11	D	11.1	4.24	11	L
OVER-ALL	61.0	3.92	3		15.9	4.33	3	

[63]

Table 11

Difficulty Level and Growth Rate Taxonomy of Basic Major Tonal Patterns

Aural Perception

Tonic Function

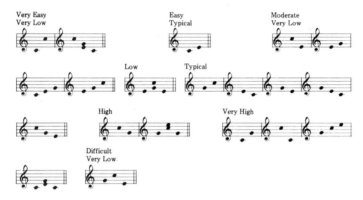

Dominant Function

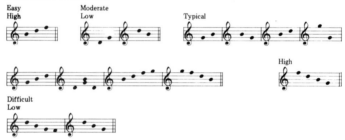

Subdominant Function

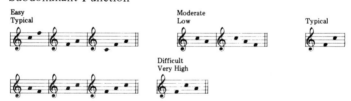

[64]

Reading Recognition

Tonic Function

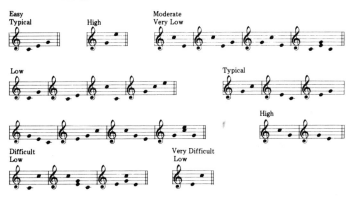

Dominant Function

Subdominant Function

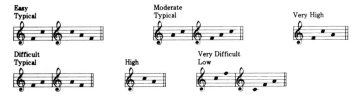

Tonic Function

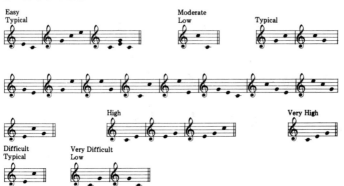

Dominant Function

Subdominant Function

Table 12

Difficulty Level and Growth Rate Taxonomy of Complex Major Tonal Patterns
Aural Perception

Chromaticism

Combined Harmonic Functions

Expanded Harmonic Functions

[67]

Chromaticism

Combined Harmonic Functions

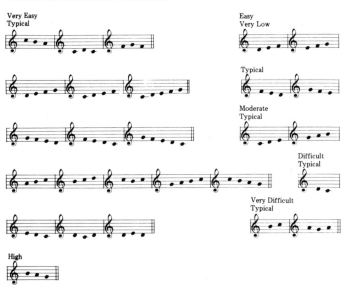

Expanded Harmonic Functions

Chromaticism

Combined Harmonic Functions

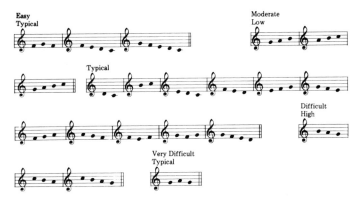

Expanded Harmonic Functions

Table 13

Difficulty Level and Growth Rate Taxonomy of Basic Minor Tonal Patterns
Aural Perception

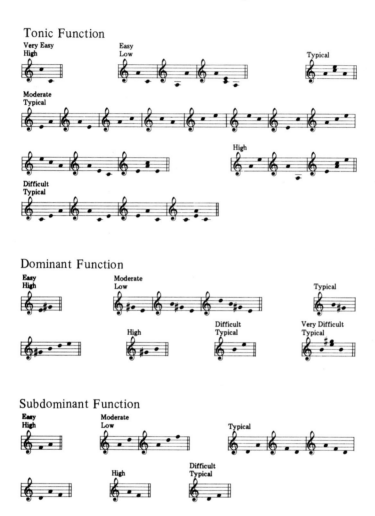

Tonic Function

Dominant Function

Subdominant Function

Reading Recognition

Tonic Function

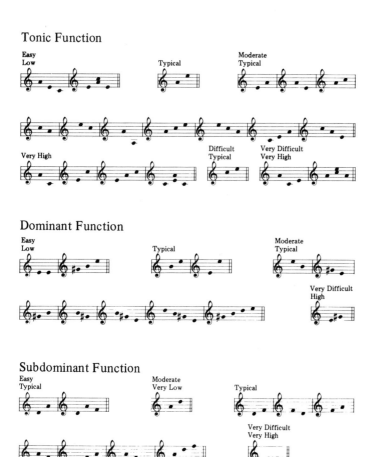

Dominant Function

Subdominant Function

Notational Understanding

Tonic Function

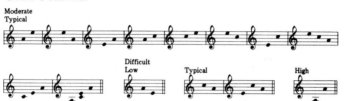

Dominant Function

Subdominant Function

Table 14

Difficulty Level and Growth Rate Taxonomy of Complex Minor Tonal Patterns
Aural Perception

Chromaticism

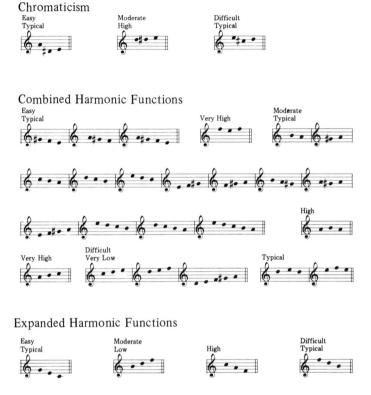

Combined Harmonic Functions

Expanded Harmonic Functions

Reading Recognition

Chromaticism

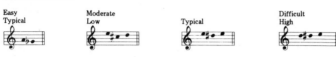

Combined Harmonic Functions

Expanded Harmonic Functions

Notational Understanding

Chromaticism

Combined Harmonic Functions

[75]

Table 15

Difficulty Level and Growth Rate Taxonomy of Basic Duple Rhythm Patterns

Aural Perception

Tempo and Meter Beats

Fractionations and Elongations

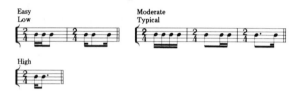

Upbeats

Tempo and Meter Beats

Fractionations and Elongations

Upbeats

Tempo and Meter Beats

Fractionations and Elongations

Upbeats

Reading Recognition

Fractionations and Elongations

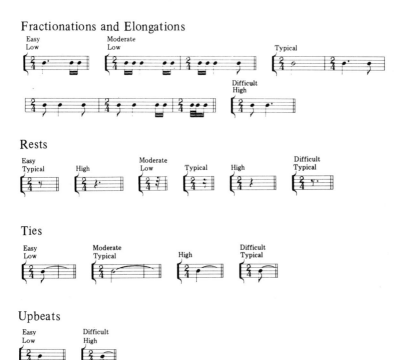

Rests

Ties

Upbeats

Table 16

Difficulty Level and Growth Rate Taxonomy of Complex Duple Rhythm Patterns

Aural Perception

Fractionations and Elongations

Ties

Upbeats

Fractionations and Elongations

Rests

Ties

Table 17

Difficulty Level and Growth Rate Taxonomy of Basic Triple Rhythm Patterns Aural Perception

Tempo and Meter Beats

Fractionations and Elongations

Upbeats

Tempo and Meter Beats

Fractionations and Elongations

Upbeats

[83]

Tempo and Meter Beats

Fractionations and Elongations

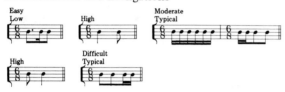

Upbeats

Table 18

Difficulty Level and Growth Rate Taxonomy of Complex Triple Rhythm Patterns

Aural Perception

Fractionations and Elongations

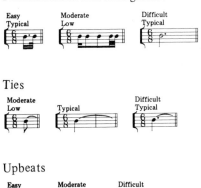

Ties

Upbeats

Fractionations and Elongations

Rests

Ties

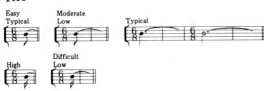

Upbeats

Rests

Easy
High

Difficult
Low

Ties

Moderate
Typical

for every tonal pattern and every rhythm pattern. Also, although the same order and sequence of the patterns as found in the Musical Organization Taxonomies in Tables 1 and 2 is maintained, the main sections of Tables 11 through 18 are structured according to *ITML* subtests (*Aural Perception, Reading Recognition,* and *Notational Understanding*) rather than according to the Musical Organization Taxonomy as in Appendixes D and E. (When studying Tables 11 through 18, it should be remembered that patterns in all Difficulty Level and Growth Rate categories were not found in every *ITML* subtest.)

To most appropriately use the tonal and rhythm patterns in Tables 11 through 18 for teaching music literacy skills in accordance with students' individual musical differences, both the musical aptitude and musical achievement of each student must be considered. That is, each student's results on the *Musical Aptitude Profile*[27] (a musical aptitude test battery) and any one complete Level of the *Iowa Tests of Music Literacy*[28] (a musical achievement test battery) should first be determined.

Percentile ranks on only the following total tests and subtests of the two batteries are needed.

Musical Aptitude Profile (Total Tests)	Iowa Tests of Music Literacy (Subtests)
Tonal Imagery (T)	Tonal Aural Perception (T1)
	Tonal Reading Recognition (T2)
	Tonal Notational Understanding (T3)
Rhythm Imagery (R)	Rhythmic Aural Perception (R1)
	Rhythmic Reading Recognition (R2)
	Rhythmic Notational Understanding (R3)

After the percentile ranks on these total tests and subtests are secured, they should be classified (for each of the eight measures) into the five divisions described below.

Percentile Ranks	Classifications
90–99	High
75–89	Above Average
25–74	Average
10–24	Below Average
1–9	Low

---

[27] Edwin Gordon, *Musical Aptitude Profile* (Boston: Houghton Mifflin, 1965).
[28] Edwin Gordon, *Iowa Tests of Music Literacy.*

Next, for each student, percentile rank classification should be separately documented for each of the following six pairs of tests.

1. *MAP* Tonal Imagery and *ITML* Tonal Aural Perception
2. *MAP* Tonal Imagery and *ITML* Tonal Reading Recognition
3. *MAP* Tonal Imagery and *ITML* Tonal Notational Understanding
4. *MAP* Rhythm Imagery and *ITML* Rhythmic Aural Perception
5. *MAP* Rhythm Imagery and *ITML* Rhythmic Reading Recognition
6. *MAP* Rhythm Imagery and *ITML* Rhythmic Notational Understanding

Then, the percentile rank classifications should be used in conjunction with Table 19. It will be noticed in Table 19 that the classifications of percentile ranks are at the top for the *Musical Aptitude Profile* and at the left for the *Iowa Tests of Music Literacy*. Above the line in each box is the Difficulty Level category for the patterns and below the line is the Growth Rate category for the patterns (as found in Tables 11 through 18).

Consider the following example:

A student is classified as Average on the *MAP Tonal Imagery* Test and as High on the *ITML* Tonal *Aural Perception* subtest. Therefore, by beginning at the bottom of the first column (from left to right) and continuing through the top of the column, and then beginning at the bottom of the second and third columns and continuing through the top of those columns (where the *MAP* Average and the *ITML* High classifications coincide), it can be determined that all tonal patterns in the combined Difficulty Level and Growth Rate categories in the fifteen boxes would be appropriate for use with that student. Specifically, for the purpose of teaching that student to hear (aurally perceive) tonal patterns, any and all patterns in the fifteen combined Difficulty Level and Growth Rate categories found under Aural Perception in Tables 11 (Basic Major Tonal Patterns), 12 (Complex Major Tonal Patterns), 13 (Basic Minor Tonal Patterns), and 14 (Complex Minor Tonal Patterns) should be utilized initially; that is, before ultimately exposing him to additional patterns which correspond to the categories in the remaining ten boxes.

For the purpose of teaching students to hear rhythm patterns, the same system should be followed but, of course, paired percentile rank classifications for the *MAP Rhythm Imagery* test and the *ITML* Rhythmic *Aural Perception* subtest should be used. Then the appropriate rhythm patterns would be identified under *Aural Perception* in Tables 15, 16, 17, and 18. Similarly, for the purposes of teaching students to read and write tonal patterns, the *MAP Tonal Imagery* percentile rank classification should be used in conjunction with *ITML* Tonal *Reading Recognition* and Tonal *Notational Understanding* percentile rank classifications respectively, and the appropriate tonal patterns should be identified under *Reading Recognition*

Table 19

Selection of Tonal and Rhythm Patterns According to Difficulty Level and Growth Rate Categories Which Correspond to Students' Classified Percentile Ranks on the *Musical Aptitude Profile* and the *Iowa Tests of Music Literacy*

		Musical Aptitude Profile			
	LOW	BELOW AVERAGE	AVERAGE	ABOVE AVERAGE	HIGH
HIGH	Very Easy* / Very Low†	Easy / Very Low	Moderate / Very Low	Difficult / Very Low	Very Difficult / Very Low
ABOVE AVERAGE	Very Easy / Low	Easy / Low	Moderate / Low	Difficult / Low	Very Difficult / Low
AVERAGE	Very Easy / Typical	Easy / Typical	Moderate / Typical	Difficult / Typical	Very Difficult / Typical
BELOW AVERAGE	Very Easy / High	Easy / High	Moderate / High	Difficult / High	Very Difficult / High
LOW	Very Easy / Very High	Easy / Very High	Moderate / Very High	Difficult / Very High	Very Difficult / Very High

(Left side label, vertical: Iowa Tests of Music Literacy*)*

* Categories above the broken line represent Difficulty Levels.
† Categories below the broken line represent Growth Rates.

(for reading) and *Notational Understanding* (for writing) in Tables 15, 16, 17, and 18.

It is suggested that the *Iowa Tests of Music Literacy Manual*[29] and the *Musical Aptitude Profile Manual*[30] be consulted for instructional techniques

---

29 Gordon, *ITML Manual,* pp. 83–94.
30 Edwin Gordon, *Musical Aptitude Profile Manual* (Boston: Houghton Mifflin, 1965), pp. 37–43.

(such as echoes, rondos, and dialogues) which may be used in combination with the patterns presented in this investigation for the purpose of teaching to students' individual musical differences in vocal and general music classes. Regarding appropriate instructional techniques which may be specifically used in instrumental music groups for similar purposes, it is recommended that Chapter Eight of *The Psychology of Music Teaching*[31] be read in detail.

A final statement would seem in order. Namely, although all possible tonal and rhythm patterns are not accounted for in this investigation and as a partial consequence, there are few, and in some cases, no patterns subsumed under given Difficulty Level and Growth Rate categories in Tables 11 through 18, these limitations should not dissuade a teacher from making appropriate use of the patterns in these tables for instructional purposes, as suggested. To the contrary, it should not be considered impermissible to infer, by studying the nature and corresponding categories of those patterns that are included in this investigation, in which Difficulty Level and Growth Rate categories the undocumented patterns might have been found if they too could have been included. Also, constraining as it might be that the design of the present investigation does not adequately provide for an explanation of the reasons why there is a lack of consistent association of a given pattern with Difficulty Level and Growth Rate categories among *ITML* subtests (within as well as between Levels), it is encouraging to remember that the categorization of the patterns does not suffer from systematic bias. That is, because the data reported in this investigation are based on the test results of a relatively large representative sample of students from across the country, the possibility that the Difficulty Level and Growth Rate categories might be contaminated by a specific type of musical instruction may be precluded.

BIBLIOGRAPHY

Apel, Willi. *Harvard Dictionary of Music*. Cambridge: Harvard University Press, 1969.
Donington, Robert. *The Interpretation of Early Music*. London: Faber and Faber, 1963.
Gordon, Edwin. *Musical Aptitude Profile*. Boston: Houghton Mifflin, 1965.
Gordon, Edwin. *Iowa Tests of Music Literacy*. Iowa City: Bureau of Educational

---

[31] Gordon, *The Psychology of Music Teaching*, pp. 120–129.

Research and Service, Division of Extension and University Services, University of Iowa, 1971.

Gordon, Edwin. *The Psychology of Music Teaching*. Englewood Cliffs: Prentice-Hall, 1971.

Palsica, Claude, ed., *Music In Our Schools*, Report of the Yale Seminar on Music Education. Washington, D.C.: Office of Education, 1964.

Smith, Frank. *Understanding Reading*. New York: Holt, Rinehart, and Winston, 1971.

APPENDIX A

Item Analysis for the Iowa Tests of Music Literacy

LEVEL I   GRADES 4–6

TONAL CONCEPTS

	Aural Perception		Reading Recognition		Notational Understanding	
	Difficulty°	Discrimination°	Difficulty	Discrimination	Difficulty	Discrimination
1.	78	14	89	22	69	32
2.	80	18	83	33	58	39
3.	37	67	67	67	68	41
4.	39	33	72	48	72	44
5.	43	11	59	67	72	37
6.	50	78	59	59	67	32
7.	48	63	80	33	56	23
8.	56	10	78	44	77	37
9.	39	70	44	37		
10.	68	18	72	33		
11.	31	56	22	10		
12.	48	89	70	37		
13.	48	59	74	52		
14.	48	96	76	26		
15.	43	85	83	26		
16.	39	26	61	63		
17.	39	56	87	22		
18.	46	48	76	48		
19.	37	44	74	52		
20.	52	67	80	33		
21.	44	81	72	56		
22.	48	74	72	48		

° Decimals have been deleted from this and following indexes.

RHYTHMIC CONCEPTS

	Aural Perception		Reading Recognition		Notational Understanding	
	Difficulty°	Discrimination°	Difficulty	Discrimination	Difficulty	Discrimination
1.	76	33	59	59	71	25
2.	83	33	72	56	62	16
3.	43	63	59	37	51	10
4.	54	48	61	56	48	10
5.	72	37	61	33	54	23
6.	67	26	54	41	57	10
7.	64	44	69	33	57	12
8.	48	37	69	48	54	13
9.	43	33	74	30	57	32
10.	32	11	44	10	62	30
11.	50	33	72	33	60	23
12.	61	37	63	59	56	21
13.	65	52	52	30	58	15
14.	65	30	26	37	40	15
15.	32	11	59	22		
16.	43	10	48	59		
17.	48	30	50	41		
18.	67	33	28	18		
19.	61	26	52	30		
20.	52	22	46	48		
21.	33	30	76	11		
22.	65	48	56	10		

LEVEL 1   GRADES 7–9

TONAL CONCEPTS

	Aural Perception Difficulty°	Discrimination°	Reading Recognition Difficulty	Discrimination	Notational Understanding Difficulty	Discrimination
1.	85	15	95	10	81	34
2.	87	10	91	19	73	39
3.	46	85	96	10	81	33
4.	57	48	96	10	80	40
5.	80	22	76	48	81	38
6.	54	93	67	67	76	41
7.	54	59	89	15	76	41
8.	69	11	87	19	87	26
9.	52	63	72	41		
10.	82	30	87	26		
11.	48	67	37	59		
12.	52	82	82	37		
13.	56	67	87	19		
14.	57	78	83	33		
15.	52	74	89	11		
16.	43	48	85	30		
17.	50	85	89	10		
18.	57	63	83	33		
19.	61	59	93	15		
20.	57	78	94	11		
21.	59	82	78	44		
22.	57	70	91	10		

RHYTHMIC CONCEPTS

	Aural Perception Difficulty°	Discrimination°	Reading Recognition Difficulty	Discrimination	Notational Understanding Difficulty	Discrimination
1.	83	33	74	41	80	33
2.	96	10	82	37	68	28
3.	65	56	72	56	66	26
4.	59	44	83	33	59	35
5.	76	41	76	48	66	31
6.	69	44	61	63	70	15
7.	69	52	74	41	70	33
8.	50	26	76	48	66	31
9.	67	44	78	44	67	51
10.	48	15	62	37	69	17
11.	57	41	78	44	67	29
12.	67	26	82	37	64	21
13.	67	56	70	52	62	25
14.	67	52	69	56	47	20
15.	59	37	69	11		
16.	56	52	63	74		
17.	63	37	70	59		
18.	69	52	63	59		
19.	70	37	74	44		
20.	54	56	74	52		
21.	50	41	80	19		
22.	70	33	66	11		

TONAL CONCEPTS

	Aural Perception		Reading Recognition		Notational Understanding	
	Difficulty°	Discrimination°	Difficulty	Discrimination	Difficulty	Discrimination
1.	89	22	96	10	89	21
2.	94	11	94	11	79	41
3.	54	93	98	10	90	20
4.	72	48	98	15	93	14
5.	82	30	87	26	92	15
6.	61	78	78	44	84	31
7.	70	52	96	10	83	33
8.	72	48	89	22	93	15
9.	54	82	74	52		
10.	93	15	89	22		
11.	50	82	63	74		
12.	59	74	89	22		
13.	61	63	91	19		
14.	67	59	87	26		
15.	56	59	94	22		
16.	61	56	87	26		
17.	61	78	90	22		
18.	59	67	93	15		
19.	63	63	96	10		
20.	59	82	96	10		
21.	65	70	91	20		
22.	63	74	96	20		

RHYTHMIC CONCEPTS

	Aural Perception		Reading Recognition		Notational Understanding	
	Difficulty°	Discrimination°	Difficulty	Discrimination	Difficulty	Discrimination
1.	85	22	80	44	91	18
2.	98	10	91	19	82	27
3.	68	52	74	48	73	42
4.	72	19	91	19	69	45
5.	82	41	85	30	72	33
6.	70	52	76	48	72	23
7.	70	30	80	52	73	33
8.	67	44	80	41	72	37
9.	69	56	85	30	77	44
10.	50	56	63	74	72	32
11.	59	44	89	22	73	28
12.	70	10	84	41	72	28
13.	87	11	80	33	68	24
14.	70	48	74	52	53	13
15.	60	70	80	33		
16.	61	70	70	52		
17.	69	52	72	56		
18.	78	44	65	74		
19.	76	33	76	56		
20.	72	19	78	44		
21.	59	74	82	37		
22.	83	19	68	33		

TONAL CONCEPTS

	Aural Perception		Reading Recognition		Notational Understanding	
	Difficulty°	Discrimination°	Difficulty	Discrimination	Difficulty	Discrimination
1.	52	30	70	59	66	38
2.	46	10	67	52	55	12
3.	48	44	78	37	57	31
4.	32	26	69	56	62	44
5.	50	26	70	19	57	29
6.	39	33	65	33	61	35
7.	63	15	72	41	70	40
8.	39	33	37	52	54	10
9.	52	37	63	67		
10.	48	26	83	19		
11.	43	33	72	41		
12.	46	41	44	30		
13.	44	37	74	44		
14.	48	44	22	15		
15.	44	30	76	33		
16.	54	33	37	22		
17.	57	26	59	74		
18.	63	15	70	59		
19.	41	37	57	41		
20.	44	30	70	52		
21.	48	30	72	56		
22.	44	52	80	10		

RHYTHMIC CONCEPTS

	Aural Perception		Reading Recognition		Notational Understanding	
	Difficulty°	Discrimination°	Difficulty	Discrimination	Difficulty	Discrimination
1.	48	30	26	11	52	13
2.	65	56	70	37	60	10
3.	57	41	74	44	56	10
4.	41	30	63	52	57	10
5.	65	33	70	22	46	16
6.	43	26	69	33	28	25
7.	52	59	52	30	27	14
8.	32	10	57	56	33	26
9.	48	59	62	33	23	20
10.	54	48	39	10	27	22
11.	44	22	56	10	27	20
12.	54	26	48	22		
13.	44	37	74	37		
14.	54	41	72	30		
15.	46	52	59	33		
16.	50	26	46	10		
17.	57	33	52	22		
18.	52	30	41	44		
19.	37	22	46	19		
20.	32	11	44	37		
21.	37	22	52	59		
22.	54	41	54	56		

TONAL CONCEPTS

	Aural Perception		Reading Recognition		Notational Understanding	
	Difficulty°	Discrimination°	Difficulty	Discrimination	Difficulty	Discrimination
1.	74	30	72	56	76	32
2.	48	48	74	22	59	23
3.	63	52	89	15	68	34
4.	52	44	82	37	78	39
5.	52	63	83	22	68	36
6.	57	41	82	30	77	36
7.	65	22	83	11	75	42
8.	48	30	52	67	56	16
9.	69	48	74	52		
10.	54	44	85	52		
11.	49	59	83	26		
12.	67	19	69	56		
13.	62	33	82	37		
14.	50	48	57	48		
15.	59	59	87	19		
16.	56	48	50	41		
17.	59	19	76	48		
18.	72	22	72	33		
19.	43	41	74	30		
20.	55	33	91	15		
21.	52	59	91	19		
22.	65	56	82	26		

RHYTHMIC CONCEPTS

	Aural Perception		Reading Recognition		Notational Understanding	
	Difficulty°	Discrimination°	Difficulty	Discrimination	Difficulty	Discrimination
1.	59	59	47	37	58	24
2.	72	41	72	48	62	13
3.	80	30	82	37	58	11
4.	44	22	69	37	62	24
5.	70	48	73	37	48	17
6.	44	44	70	48	31	27
7.	59	52	72	33	32	13
8.	39	33	76	19	34	25
9.	50	56	67	37	26	19
10.	56	48	52	22	29	23
11.	52	37	58	56	32	21
12.	59	33	70	59		
13.	52	67	80	11		
14.	57	22	79	41		
15.	57	30	65	44		
16.	57	41	57	10		
17.	70	41	67	44		
18.	54	52	48	52		
19.	57	41	63	44		
20.	44	52	67	59		
21.	41	11	54	63		
22.	67	30	56	33		

TONAL CONCEPTS

	Aural Perception		Reading Recognition		Notational Understanding	
	Difficulty°	Discrimination°	Difficulty	Discrimination	Difficulty	Discrimination
1.	85	22	96	10	83	31
2.	67	15	98	10	73	30
3.	76	41	91	22	75	44
4.	56	67	93	15	84	28
5.	76	33	89	22	77	37
6.	59	48	96	10	79	41
7.	67	63	96	10	83	32
8.	56	22	74	52	69	20
9.	72	56	89	22		
10.	78	15	87	33		
11.	59	67	93	15		
12.	80	67	76	48		
13.	67	67	93	15		
14.	74	30	63	74		
15.	87	26	89	22		
16.	64	30	70	59		
17.	62	10	89	22		
18.	89	63	89	22		
19.	69	33	87	26		
20.	66	33	93	19		
21.	72	48	96	10		
22.	78	44	83	37		

RHYTHMIC CONCEPTS

	Aural Perception		Reading Recognition		Notational Understanding	
	Difficulty°	Discrimination°	Difficulty	Discrimination	Difficulty	Discrimination
1.	80	41	67	37	64	22
2.	76	48	91	19	63	14
3.	83	41	91	19	63	22
4.	69	48	70	59	71	19
5.	72	59	89	22	55	16
6.	57	85	89	22	32	24
7.	78	44	80	33	37	14
8.	56	67	80	33	40	18
9.	52	82	69	56	30	16
10.	57	70	65	70	30	18
11.	54	19	70	37	33	20
12.	57	33	78	44		
13.	59	67	94	11		
14.	59	70	96	10		
15.	66	70	87	26		
16.	69	33	74	44		
17.	72	44	76	48		
18.	69	41	61	70		
19.	60	56	78	37		
20.	59	74	74	52		
21.	43	37	83	19		
22.	80	33	63	44		

LEVEL 3 GRADES 4–6

TONAL CONCEPTS

	Aural Perception		Reading Recognition		Notational Understanding	
	Difficulty°	Discrimination°	Difficulty	Discrimination	Difficulty	Discrimination
1.	50	41	65	56	80	26
2.	69	41	70	59	66	27
3.	43	37	70	59	69	30
4.	50	33	83	26	71	37
5.	63	52	70	44	63	22
6.	61	52	48	30	69	43
7.	50	41	80	33	68	37
8.	41	33	74	26		
9.	52	44	57	56		
10.	44	67	62	15		
11.	61	48	37	30		
12.	61	41	78	37		
13.	31	19	82	30		
14.	61	48	67	52		
15.	54	26	13	10		
16.	53	44	76	41		
17.	43	41	57	70		
18.	54	56	74	52		
19.	67	37	59	44		
20.	56	44	69	48		
21.	48	37	67	52		
22.	52	52	82	22		

RHYTHMIC CONCEPTS

	Aural Perception		Reading Recognition		Notational Understanding	
	Difficulty°	Discrimination°	Difficulty	Discrimination	Difficulty	Discrimination
1.	65	33	59	30	65	21
2.	60	37	52	30	67	31
3.	46	30	44	44	65	14
4.	65	56	54	48	61	23
5.	24	10	54	41	56	19
6.	44	37	20	19	53	14
7.	35	48	46	41	57	19
8.	46	56	44	30	69	24
9.	70	44	50	33	62	11
10.	22	10	57	41	58	21
11.	64	44	31	30	67	35
12.	72	48	41	26		
13.	69	26	70	37		
14.	63	37	50	33		
15.	48	37	52	30		
16.	48	52	61	48		
17.	61	33	56	52		
18.	80	19	41	33		
19.	70	52	57	10		
20.	59	37	41	44		
21.	52	30	46	48		
22.	54	33	44	15		

LEVEL 3   GRADES 7–9

TONAL CONCEPTS

	Aural Perception Difficulty°	Aural Perception Discrimination°	Reading Recognition Difficulty	Reading Recognition Discrimination	Notational Understanding Difficulty	Notational Understanding Discrimination
1.	74	37	82	37	83	32
2.	87	26	83	33	72	42
3.	50	41	85	30	80	34
4.	52	59	85	22	83	25
5.	70	51	72	56	74	33
6.	63	52	67	44	80	30
7.	58	37	85	22	76	29
8.	44	37	83	22		
9.	67	26	72	56		
10.	67	56	65	26		
11.	67	67	65	56		
12.	65	48	83	33		
13.	37	30	84	37		
14.	63	44	72	56		
15.	58	52	19	10		
16.	54	56	78	33		
17.	56	30	70	52		
18.	65	63	82	30		
19.	78	26	80	33		
20.	70	44	80	41		
21.	50	22	83	33		
22.	67	59	83	33		

RHYTHMIC CONCEPTS

	Aural Perception Difficulty°	Aural Perception Discrimination°	Reading Recognition Difficulty	Reading Recognition Discrimination	Notational Understanding Difficulty	Notational Understanding Discrimination
1.	78	10	74	30	71	23
2.	69	56	54	48	76	16
3.	56	11	69	41	68	23
4.	68	33	63	22	63	23
5.	35	41	74	44	59	10
6.	46	26	22	30	62	26
7.	44	22	52	59	59	16
8.	48	30	69	10	82	15
9.	85	10	54	19	63	14
10.	26	19	76	33	60	28
11.	70	26	37	15	71	16
12.	74	37	51	22		
13.	70	37	73	37		
14.	82	37	57	33		
15.	54	33	59	30		
16.	50	52	69	26		
17.	63	37	59	67		
18.	82	22	43	48		
19.	80	33	59	10		
20.	67	37	67	44		
21.	55	48	54	30		
22.	70	30	72	48		

TONAL CONCEPTS

	Aural Perception		Reading Recognition		Notational Understanding	
	Difficulty°	Discrimination°	Difficulty	Discrimination	Difficulty	Discrimination
1.	89	22	93	15	97	10
2.	96	10	94	11	84	31
3.	58	37	96	10	93	15
4.	58	44	87	26	88	24
5.	76	30	91	19	81	36
6.	65	48	87	26	82	34
7.	65	26	90	41	82	29
8.	52	67	87	26		
9.	72	37	87	26		
10.	69	44	69	41		
11.	74	44	82	37		
12.	71	33	87	26		
13.	54	10	88	37		
14.	70	30	83	33		
15.	63	56	26	15		
16.	59	59	80	52		
17.	61	19	87	26		
18.	78	37	89	22		
19.	87	30	97	10		
20.	74	30	89	10		
21.	57	33	94	11		
22.	74	37	87	26		

RHYTHMIC CONCEPTS

	Aural Perception		Reading Recognition		Notational Understanding	
	Difficulty°	Discrimination°	Difficulty	Discrimination	Difficulty	Discrimination
1.	93	15	91	10	73	19
2.	72	30	78	30	80	22
3.	57	26	71	10	69	34
4.	70	44	78	22	73	32
5.	44	33	89	10	65	28
6.	49	44	56	82	76	27
7.	48	22	63	44	78	17
8.	56	44	74	15	93	10
9.	89	10	57	41	69	25
10.	32	37	96	10	73	29
11.	74	48	46	41	77	14
12.	78	37	67	30		
13.	76	22	82	22		
14.	91	19	72	41		
15.	72	26	70	59		
16.	69	63	85	22		
17.	65	41	74	44		
18.	89	15	56	30		
19.	83	11	61	33		
20.	76	26	52	59		
21.	59	44	63	63		
22.	72	33	78	37		

[103]

TONAL CONCEPTS

	Aural Perception		Reading Recognition		Notational Understanding	
	Difficulty°	Discrimination°	Difficulty	Discrimination	Difficulty	Discrimination
1.	70	52	78	37	70	12
2.	70	30	85	30	43	14
3.	76	33	82	30	34	26
4.	72	41	74	30	39	15
5.	32	10	85	22	10	10
6.	80	41	61	63	30	30
7.	78	44	82	37	30	35
8.	46	10	65	56		
9.	57	33	69	56		
10.	70	44	39	48		
11.	52	37	57	26		
12.	54	15	80	19		
13.	54	41	76	26		
14.	80	41	35	11		
15.	69	44	56	30		
16.	69	33	59	37		
17.	61	56	69	41		
18.	64	48	63	37		
19.	61	48	39	33		
20.	69	56	76	33		
21.	69	41	70	52		
22.	74	37	76	33		

RHYTHMIC CONCEPTS

	Aural Perception		Reading Recognition		Notational Understanding	
	Difficulty°	Discrimination°	Difficulty	Discrimination	Difficulty	Discrimination
1.	63	74	65	41	71	11
2.	63	52	63	52	52	19
3.	69	48	70	48	54	10
4.	65	63	50	11	75	31
5.	63	44	74	44	80	13
6.	65	63	59	44	62	18
7.	63	59	24	11	63	23
8.	70	41	82	15	65	24
9.	56	59	63	59	68	12
10.	54	63	56	74	58	20
11.	63	44	46	48	64	21
12.	54	48	82	15	61	23
13.	57	48	57	26		
14.	76	33	67	37		
15.	50	33	54	63		
16.	54	48	67	48		
17.	52	52	70	26		
18.	61	41	48	52		
19.	50	48	61	56		
20.	52	52	69	48		
21.	54	78	59	44		
22.	44	59	65	56		

TONAL CONCEPTS

	Aural Perception		Reading Recognition		Notational Understanding	
	Difficulty°	Discrimination°	Difficulty	Discrimination	Difficulty	Discrimination
1.	85	22	93	15	91	19
2.	78	10	91	10	83	16
3.	91	19	85	22	71	17
4.	80	19	89	15	90	19
5.	43	20	87	26	57	10
6.	88	37	63	70	40	35
7.	85	30	83	33	41	39
8.	52	33	82	37		
9.	61	33	80	26		
10.	82	30	59	59		
11.	57	63	60	52		
12.	59	33	82	33		
13.	74	37	79	22		
14.	90	37	43	56		
15.	74	41	65	48		
16.	93	10	62	67		
17.	72	11	80	11		
18.	65	48	72	48		
19.	69	33	42	26		
20.	80	19	85	15		
21.	70	52	79	44		
22.	78	37	83	26		

RHYTHMIC CONCEPTS

	Aural Perception		Reading Recognition		Notational Understanding	
	Difficulty°	Discrimination°	Difficulty	Discrimination	Difficulty	Discrimination
1.	65	63	80	41	72	23
2.	82	37	70	30	58	27
3.	72	56	72	52	59	17
4.	76	48	61	48	78	35
5.	67	30	77	52	83	28
6.	69	48	78	37	65	23
7.	65	52	33	30	64	23
8.	72	52	85	30	70	31
9.	65	56	72	56	70	25
10.	61	56	72	41	62	22
11.	65	56	59	52	76	28
12.	61	26	93	30	64	22
13.	63	59	65	33		
14.	82	37	72	56		
15.	67	44	65	56		
16.	61	56	69	37		
17.	65	48	76	59		
18.	63	37	63	67		
19.	59	52	72	41		
20.	63	48	70	44		
21.	67	52	65	48		
22.	54	41	69	56		

LEVEL 5 GRADES 7–9

TONAL CONCEPTS

	Aural Perception		Reading Recognition		Notational Understanding	
	Difficulty°	Discrimination°	Difficulty	Discrimination	Difficulty	Discrimination
1.	52	15	39	33	63	28
2.	56	30	57	63	60	23
3.	43	33	65	30	64	25
4.	63	44	37	22	61	27
5.	41	44	35	11	72	40
6.	61	26	76	19	68	36
7.	43	41	41	37		
8.	43	41	28	26		
9.	43	33	41	52		
10.	33	10	65	19		
11.	30	22	56	22		
12.	56	30	35	19		
13.	41	52	57	56		
14.	43	48	52	22		
15.	43	48	70	26		
16.	59	44	35	10		
17.	54	19	43	30		
18.	43	33	65	33		
19.	48	44	32	11		
20.	32	19	33	19		
21.	46	63	44	52		
22.	44	67	59	30		

RHYTHMIC CONCEPTS

	Aural Perception		Reading Recognition		Notational Understanding	
	Difficulty°	Discrimination°	Difficulty	Discrimination	Difficulty	Discrimination
1.	50	48	69	26	67	32
2.	65	48	67	37	59	28
3.	50	41	67	37	71	39
4.	56	59	67	37	57	28
5.	30	48	63	30	73	38
6.	63	37	52	30	66	37
7.	32	44	32	33	58	19
8.	33	52	30	30	63	34
9.	50	63	43	33	71	42
10.	54	59	65	11		
11.	65	48	52	37		
12.	63	67	69	48		
13.	20	56	43	56		
14.	57	56	54	26		
15.	50	33	48	37		
16.	54	63	70	44		
17.	56	59	56	59		
18.	63	44	61	56		
19.	54	41	57	41		
20.	69	48	54	41		
21.	56	37	65	26		
22.	54	41	48	67		

TONAL CONCEPTS

	Aural Perception		Reading Recognition		Notational Understanding	
	Difficulty°	Discrimination°	Difficulty	Discrimination	Difficulty	Discrimination
1.	80	26	50	70	75	43
2.	80	19	74	52	73	40
3.	56	67	67	26	73	37
4.	74	52	48	44	75	45
5.	54	41	39	10	80	37
6.	72	41	83	26	79	36
7.	54	33	63	30		
8.	48	30	61	33		
9.	65	63	70	52		
10.	50	33	87	26		
11.	46	26	78	37		
12.	76	41	63	67		
13.	52	30	61	56		
14.	50	70	65	48		
15.	70	59	73	19		
16.	74	44	39	33		
17.	80	33	48	48		
18.	65	56	80	33		
19.	57	48	33	10		
20.	43	41	35	59		
21.	52	44	70	37		
22.	74	52	71	22		

RHYTHMIC CONCEPTS

	Aural Perception		Reading Recognition		Notational Understanding	
	Difficulty°	Discrimination°	Difficulty	Discrimination	Difficulty	Discrimination
1.	54	56	83	33	83	32
2.	67	44	80	41	69	31
3.	55	33	74	44	74	40
4.	63	52	85	30	72	49
5.	50	44	78	37	76	36
6.	67	52	67	37	71	42
7.	52	26	56	52	63	26
8.	56	30	65	41	73	42
9.	61	63	52	82	77	45
10.	56	26	76	48		
11.	67	59	76	48		
12.	78	37	85	22		
13.	46	26	59	52		
14.	70	52	65	10		
15.	75	52	80	41		
16.	57	56	85	10		
17.	65	56	58	67		
18.	65	52	78	44		
19.	57	78	65	41		
20.	72	48	67	59		
21.	58	74	69	41		
22.	65	56	78	37		

TONAL CONCEPTS

	Aural Perception		Reading Recognition		Notational Understanding	
	Difficulty°	Discrimination°	Difficulty	Discrimination	Difficulty	Discrimination
1.	69	56	37	44	45	21
2.	70	37	54	48	72	30
3.	65	26	33	37	58	27
4.	50	26	52	10	59	24
5.	56	67	50	33	52	12
6.	69	26	71	33	52	26
7.	62	56	59	59	55	13
8.	63	52	57	26	50	12
9.	61	78	44	44		
10.	67	48	52	33		
11.	61	41	46	33		
12.	61	56	54	19		
13.	70	52	52	44		
14.	56	52	50	19		
15.	61	63	39	48		
16.	64	56	22	30		
17.	63	67	37	15		
18.	63	52	44	52		
19.	61	48	56	30		
20.	70	37	63	33		
21.	61	48	50	48		
22.	54	41	59	22		

RHYTHMIC CONCEPTS

	Aural Perception		Reading Recognition		Notational Understanding	
	Difficulty°	Discrimination°	Difficulty	Discrimination	Difficulty	Discrimination
1.	52	26	63	67	59	18
2.	72	48	70	15	63	19
3.	63	30	43	26	59	11
4.	67	52	59	37	62	15
5.	61	59	72	41	51	11
6.	54	63	67	30	55	20
7.	46	63	63	30	61	20
8.	41	52	32	19	56	18
9.	67	67	46	33	62	26
10.	50	41	67	37	63	21
11.	82	37	67	44		
12.	50	63	76	33		
13.	61	59	59	56		
14.	74	37	74	44		
15.	74	44	37	48		
16.	65	26	50	56		
17.	65	41	70	44		
18.	61	56	50	56		
19.	63	52	37	37		
20.	61	63	54	33		
21.	61	33	69	11		
22.	67	52	70	37		

TONAL CONCEPTS

	Aural Perception		Reading Recognition		Notational Understanding	
	Difficulty°	Discrimination°	Difficulty	Discrimination	Difficulty	Discrimination
1.	70	52	43	63	46	22
2.	82	15	63	52	74	30
3.	72	48	50	63	67	35
4.	64	41	61	11	70	32
5.	61	78	59	37	59	20
6.	71	67	72	41	54	27
7.	65	82	72	33	60	18
8.	67	59	73	41	70	28
9.	64	70	46	56		
10.	69	78	54	22		
11.	63	59	63	59		
12.	64	56	76	19		
13.	78	44	70	44		
14.	67	44	52	30		
15.	67	78	46	63		
16.	65	85	44	15		
17.	67	67	48	10		
18.	65	48	52	52		
19.	69	33	63	10		
20.	74	52	69	37		
21.	67	56	61	55		
22.	80	33	80	10		

RHYTHMIC CONCEPTS

	Aural Perception		Reading Recognition		Notational Understanding	
	Difficulty°	Discrimination°	Difficulty	Discrimination	Difficulty	Discrimination
1.	57	59	65	63	66	11
2.	82	30	78	37	64	17
3.	65	52	57	33	63	10
4.	69	78	69	52	68	24
5.	67	56	80	41	59	16
6.	69	56	70	30	67	27
7.	54	33	69	33	64	24
8.	57	70	48	15	57	16
9.	69	63	59	30	67	31
10.	59	59	70	30	65	20
11.	84	37	72	41		
12.	57	70	77	37		
13.	67	71	65	22		
14.	76	37	77	37		
15.	82	37	54	30		
16.	69	26	60	56		
17.	69	63	74	52		
18.	63	59	52	59		
19.	80	33	57	26		
20.	69	48	61	56		
21.	65	63	78	44		
22.	69	56	76	41		

APPENDIX B

Basic Major Tonal Patterns
Tonic Function

Number	Level Pattern	Level Test ITML	Item	Difficulty 4-6	Difficulty 7-9	Difficulty 10-12	Difficulty Comp.	Difficulty Growth	Over-all Diff.	Over-all Growth	Category Diff.	Category Growth
1		2-1		44	65	78	62	34	62	34	M	VH
		2-2 T-B		76	87	89	84	13	84	13	M	L
		4-3			30	41	36	11	36	11	VD	L
2		4-3			30	41	36	11	36	11	VD	L
3		1-1		37	61	63	54	26				
		1-1		48	57	63	56	15				
		2-1		46	67	80	64	34	63	23	M	T
		4-1			70	85	78	15				
		1-2 T-B		89	95	96	93	7				
		1-2 T		67	96	98	87	31				
		1-2 T		59	67	78	68	19				
		1-2 B		44	72	74	63	30				
		2-2 T-B		70	83	89	81	19	78	19	M	T
		2-2 T		72	83	93	83	21				
		2-2 TB		76	87	89	84	13				

Number	Pattern	Level Test ITML	Item	Difficulty 4-6	7-9	10-12	Comp.	Growth	Over-all Diff.	Growth	Category Diff.	Growth
		3-2 T		70	85	96	84	26				
		4-2 T			61	63	62	2				
		1-3		68	81	90	80	22				
		1-3		77	87	93	86	16				
		2-3		54	56	69	60	15	74	22	M	T
		3-3		71	83	88	81	17				
		4-3			43	83	63	40				
4		1-1		37	61	63	54	26				
		2-1		48	63	76	62	28				
		2-1		46	67	80	64	34	61	25	M	H
		2-1		48	50	74	57	26				
		3-1		63	70	76	70	13				
		1-2 T		67	96	98	87	31				
		1-2 T		76	83	87	82	11				
		1-2 T		61	85	87	78	26				
		1-2 B		44	72	74	63	30	80	23	M	H
		2-2 T-B		78	89	91	86	13				
		2-2 B		70	72	96	79	26				
		3-2 T-B		70	85	96	84	26				
		1-3		77	87	93	86	16				
		2-3		55	59	73	62	18				
		2-3		70	75	83	76	13	71	16	M	T
		2-3		54	56	69	60	15				

Number	Pattern	Level Test ITML	Item	Difficulty 4-6	7-9	10-12	Comp.	Growth	Over-all Diff.	Over-all Growth	Category Diff.	Category Growth
5	[music]	1-1	[music]	78	85	89	84	11				
		2-1	[music]	44	65	78	62	34	71	21	E	T
		3-1	[music]	56	70	74	67	18				
		1-2 B	[music]	67	96	98	87	31				
		2-2 T-B	[music]	83	85	87	85	4				
		2-2 T-B	[music]	76	87	89	84	13	84	15	M	L
		2-2 T-B	[music]	70	91	93	85	21				
		3-2 T	[music]	76	78	80	78	4				
		1-3	[music]	72	81	92	82	20				
		1-3	[music]	56	76	83	72	27				
		3-3	[music]	63	74	81	73	18	65	28	M	H
		4-3	[music]		43	83	63	40				
		4-3	[music]		39	90	65	51				
		4-3	[music]		30	41	36	11				
6	[music]	1-1	[music]	39	50	61	50	22				
		1-1	[music]	48	57	63	56	15				
		2-1	[music]	48	63	76	62	28				
		2-1	[music]	48	50	74	57	26				
		2-1	[music]	44	55	66	55	22	63	21	M	T
		2-1	[music]	44	65	78	62	34				
		3-1	[music]	52	67	72	64	20				
		4-1	[music]		76	91	84	15				
		4-1	[music]		69	80	75	11				

Number	Pattern	Level Test ITML	Item	Difficulty 4-6	7-9	10-12	Comp.	Growth	Over-all Diff.	Growth	Category Diff.	Growth
		1-2 T-B		89	95	96	93	7				
		1-2 T-B		80	94	96	90	16				
		2-2 T-B		78	89	91	86	13				
		2-2 T-B		22	57	63	47	41				
		2-2 T-B		76	87	89	84	13				
		2-2 B		70	72	96	79	26	74	21	M	T
		3-2 T		59	80	97	79	38				
		3-2 B		37	65	82	61	45				
		4-2 T-B			85	87	86	2				
		4-2 T-B			65	82	74	17				
		4-2 T-B			35	43	39	8				
		1-3		77	87	93	86	16	80	17	E	T
		3-3		63	74	81	73	18				
7		4-2 T			30	40	35	10	35	10	VD	L
		2-3		55	59	73	62	18				
		2-3		54	56	69	60	15	53	15	D	T
		4-3			30	41	36	11				
8		1-1		48	57	63	56	15	66	13	M	VL
		4-1			69	80	75	11				
		1-2 T-B		89	95	96	93	7				
		4-2 T-B			61	63	62	2	67	9	M	VL
		4-2 T			65	82	74	17				
		4-2 T-B			35	43	39	8				

[116]

Number	Pattern	ITML (Level Test)	Item	4-6	7-9	10-12	Comp.	Growth	Diff. (Over-all)	Growth (Over-all)	Diff. (Category)	Growth (Category)
9	[music notation]	1-1	[music notation]	78	85	89	84	11				
		1-1	[music notation]	48	57	63	56	15				
		2-1	[music notation]	48	63	76	62	28				
		2-1	[music notation]	39	48	56	48	17	64	16	M	VL
		2-1	[music notation]	43	49	59	50	16				
		3-1	[music notation]	63	70	76	70	13				
		4-1	[music notation]		70	85	78	15				
		1-2 T-B	[music notation]	89	95	96	93	7				
		1-2 T-B	[music notation]	59	67	87	71	28				
		1-2 T-B	[music notation]	22	37	63	41	41				
		1-2 B	[music notation]	67	96	98	87	31				
		1-2 B	[music notation]	61	85	87	78	26				
		2-2 T-B	[music notation]	83	85	87	85	4	77	20	M	T
		2-2 T-B	[music notation]	70	91	93	85	23				
		2-2 T-B	[music notation]	80	82	83	82	3				
		2-2 B	[music notation]	70	72	96	79	26				
		3-2 T	[music notation]	70	85	96	84	26				
		4-2 T	[music notation]		61	63	62	2				
		1-3	[music notation]	68	81	90	80	22				
		1-3	[music notation]	56	76	83	72	27	72	33	M	H
		4-3	[music notation]		39	90	65	51				

Number	Pattern	Level Test ITML	Item	Difficulty 4-6	7-9	10-12	Comp.	Growth	Over-all Diff.	Growth	Category Diff.	Growth
10	♪	1-1	♪	39	57	72	56	33				
		1-1	♪	39	50	61	50	22				
		1-1	♪	37	61	63	54	26				
		1-1	♪	48	57	63	56	15				
		2-1	♪	48	63	76	62	28				
		2-1	♪	48	50	74	57	26				
		2-1	♪	44	55	66	55	22	64	20	M	T
		3-1	♪	52	67	72	64	20				
		3-1	♪	61	63	70	65	9				
		3-1	♪	67	78	87	77	20				
		4-1	♪		76	98	84	15				
		4-1	♪		78	85	82	7				
		1-2 T-B	♪	89	95	96	93	7				
		1-2 T	♪	22	37	63	41	41				
		1-2 T	♪	76	83	87	82	11				
		1-2 T	♪	74	93	96	88	22				
		1-2 T-B	♪	80	94	96	90	16				
		1-2 B	♪	59	67	78	68	19				
		1-2 B	♪	44	72	74	63	30				
		2-2 T-B	♪	78	89	91	86	13	73	22	M	H
		2-2 T-B	♪	22	57	63	47	41				
		2-2 B	♪	70	72	96	79	26				
		3-2 T-B	♪	37	65	82	61	45				
		3-2 B	♪	70	85	96	84	26				

Number	Level			Difficulty					Over-all		Category	
	Pattern	Test ITML	Item	4-6	7-9	10-12	Comp.	Growth	Diff.	Growth	Diff.	Growth
		4-2 T-B			85	87	86	2				
		4-2 T-B			69	80	74	11				
		4-2 T			39	59	49	20				
		1-3		56	76	83	72	27				
		2-3		55	59	73	62	18	71	21	M	T
		2-3		62	78	84	75	22				
		3-3		63	74	81	73	18				
11		2-2 B		72	91	96	86	24	86	24	E	H
		2-3		54	56	69	60	15	60	15	M	T
12		3-3		68	72	82	75	14	75	14	M	T
13		4-1			69	80	75	11	75	11	VE	VL
		4-2 T-B			65	82	74	17	57	13	D	L
		4-2 T-B			35	43	39	8				
		2-3		54	56	69	60	15	60	15	M	T
14		2-1		44	65	78	62	34	62	34	M	VH
		2-2 T-B		76	87	89	84	13	84	13	M	L
		3-3		63	74	81	73	18	56	12	M	L
		4-3			35	41	38	6				
16		2-3		54	56	69	60	**15**	60	15	M	T

Number	Level Pattern	Level ITML	Item	Difficulty 4-6	7-9	10-12	Comp.	Growth	Over-all Diff.	Growth	Category Diff.	Growth
19	𝄞 (music)	1-1	(music)	78	85	89	84	11				
		2-1	(music)	39	48	56	48	17	65	15	M	VL
		2-1	(music)	43	49	59	50	16				
		4-1	(music)		70	85	78	15				
		1-2 B	(music)	67	96	98	87	31				
		2-2 T	(music)	83	85	87	85	4	86	19	E	T
		2-2 T-B	(music)	70	91	93	85	23				
		4-3	(music)		43	83	63	40	64	46	M	VH
		4-3	(music)		39	90	65	51				
20	𝄞 (music)	1-1	(music)	39	50	61	50	22				
		1-1	(music)	48	57	63	56	15				
		2-1	(music)	48	63	76	62	28				
		2-1	(music)	48	50	74	57	26	61	21	M	T
		2-1	(music)	44	55	66	55	22				
		3-1	(music)	52	67	72	64	20				
		4-1	(music)		76	91	84	15				
		1-2 T-B	(music)	89	95	96	93	7				
		1-2 T	(music)	76	83	87	82	11				
		1-2 T-B	(music)	80	94	96	90	16				
		2-2 T-B	(music)	78	89	91	86	13	78	20	M	T
		2-2 T-B	(music)	22	57	63	47	41				

[120]

Number	Pattern	Level Test ITML	Item	4-6	7-9	10-12	Comp.	Growth	Diff.	Growth	Diff.	Growth
		2-2 B		70	72	96	79	26				
		3-2 B		37	65	82	61	45				
		4-2 T-B			85	87	86	2				
		3-3		63	74	81	73	18	73	18	M	T
21		1-1		48	57	63	56	15	67	15	M	VL
		4-1			70	85	78	15				
		1-2 T-B		89	95	96	93	7				
		1-2 T		59	67	78	68	19	82	18	M	T
		2-2 B		70	83	89	81	19				
		3-2 T		70	85	96	84	26				
		1-3		56	76	83	72	27	68	34	M	H
		4-3			43	83	63	40				
22		1-1		51	61	63	54	26	61	23	M	T
		2-1		48	63	76	62	28				
		2-1		48	50	74	57	26				
		3-1		63	70	76	70	13				
		1-2 T		76	83	87	82	11				
		1-2 B		44	72	74	63	30				
		2-2 T-B		78	89	91	86	13	79	21	M	T
		2-2 B		70	72	96	79	26				
		3-2 B		70	85	96	84	26				

[121]

Number	Level			Difficulty					Over-all		Category	
	Pattern	ITML Test	Item	4-6	7-9	10-12	Comp.	Growth	Diff.	Growth	Diff.	Growth
		2-3		55	59	73	62	18	62	18	M	T
23		2-1		44	65	78	62	34	62	34	M	VH
		2-2 T-B		76	87	89	84	13	84	13	M	L
		3-3		71	83	88	81	17	81	17	E	T
24		1-3		56	76	83	72	27	72	27	M	T
31		1-2 B		89	95	96	93	7	77	4	M	VL
		4-2 T		61	63	62	2					
33		1-1		48	57	63	56	15	56	15	D	VL
		1-2 T		89	95	96	93	7	78	5	M	VL
		4-2 T			61	63	62	2				
34		2-3		55	59	73	62	18	62	18	M	T
38		4-1			69	80	75	11	75	11	VE	VL
		4-2 T-B			65	82	74	17	57	13	D	L
		4-2 T-B			35	43	39	8				
43		2-1		44	65	78	62	34	62	34	M	VH
		2-2 B		76	87	89	84	13	73	8	M	VL
		4-2 T			61	63	62	2				
		1-3		77	87	93	86	16	86	16	E	T

Number	Pattern	Level Test ITML	Item	Difficulty 4-6	7-9	10-12	Comp.	Growth	Over-all Diff.	Over-all Growth	Category Diff.	Category Growth
44	♪	1-1	♪	48	57	63	56	15	67	18	M	L
		3-1	♪	67	78	87	77	20				
		1-2 T-B	♪	89	95	96	93	7	59	15	D	L
		1-2 T	♪	22	37	63	41	41				
		4-2 T	♪		61	63	62	2				
		4-2 T	♪		35	43	39	8				
45	♪	2-1	♪	46	67	80	64	34	67	24	M	H
		3-1	♪	63	70	76	70	13				
		1-2 T	♪	89	96	98	94	9	81	17	M	T
		1-2 B	♪	44	72	74	63	30				
		2-2 T	♪	80	82	83	82	3				
		3-2 T	♪	70	85	96	84	26				

Basic Major Tonal Patterns
Dominant Function

Number	Pattern	Level Test ITML	Item	4-6	7-9	10-12	Comp.	Growth	Over-all Diff.	Over-all Growth	Category Diff.	Category Growth
3	[music]	1-1	[music]	43	80	82	68	39				
		2-1	[music]	63	65	68	65	5	64	16	M	L
		2-1	[music]	57	59	62	59	5				
5	[music]	2-1	[music]	48	63	76	62	28	63	31	M	T
			[music]	46	67	80	64	34				
		2-2 T-B	[music]	80	82	83	82	3	81	15	M	T
		2-2 T	[music]	70	72	96	79	26				
		1-3	[music]	58	73	79	70	21	67	31	M	T
		4-3	[music]		43	83	63	40				
6	[music]	1-1	[music]	48	52	59	53	11				
		2-1	[music]	46	67	80	64	34	65	28	M	T
		2-1	[music]	44	59	87	63	43				
		4-1	[music]		69	93	81	24				
		1-2 T	[music]	59	67	78	68	19				
		1-2 T-B	[music]	87	89	90	89	3	80	8	M	L
		2-2 T-B	[music]	80	82	83	82	3				
8	[music]	3-2 T	[music]	37	65	82	61	45	61	45	D	VH

Number	Pattern	Level Test ITML	Item	4-6	7-9	10-12	Comp.	Growth	Over-all Diff.	Over-all Growth	Category Diff.	Category Growth
9	♪	1-1	♪	48	54	70	57	22				
		2-1	♪	50	52	76	59	26				
		2-1	♪	46	67	80	64	34	61	21	M	T
		3-1	♪		61	63	62	2				
		1-2 T	♪	67	96	98	87	31				
		2-2 B	♪	80	82	83	82	3	81	17	M	T
		4-2 T-B	♪		65	82	74	17				
		4-3	♪		10	57	35	47	37	47	VD	VH
10	♪	1-1	♪	48	54	70	57	22				
		1-1	♪	48	52	59	53	11				
		4-1	♪		70	82	76	12	61	13	M	L
		4-1	♪		54	59	57	5				
		1-2 T-B	♪	87	89	90	89	3				
		2-2 B	♪	72	78	91	80	19	85	11	M	T
14	♪	2-1	♪	44	65	78	62	34	62	34	M	T
		2-2 T-B	♪	67	87	89	81	22	81	22	M	T
19	♪	3-2 T	♪	59	80	97	79	38	79	38	M	H
20	♪	2-2 T	♪	22	57	63	47	41	47	41	VD	H
22	♪	2-1	♪	46	67	80	64	34	64	34	M	T
		2-2 T-B	♪	80	82	83	82	3	82	3	M	VL

[125]

Number	Level			Difficulty					Over-all		Category	
	Pattern	Test ITML	Item	4-6	7-9	10-12	Comp.	Growth	Diff.	Growth	Diff.	Growth
23		1-1		48	52	59	53	11				
		2-1		44	59	87	63	43	56	24	D	T
		3-1		43	56	61	53	18				
		1-2 T-B		87	89	90	89	3	89	3	E	VL
24		1-1		43	80	82	68	39	68	39	E	H
		1-2 T-B		74	87	91	84	17	84	17	M	T
48		1-1		48	54	70	57	22	57	22	M	T
		1-2 B		61	85	87	78	26	78	26	M	T
50		2-1		44	59	87	63	43	63	43	M	H
		2-2 B		72	91	96	86	24	86	24	M	T
51		2-1		50	52	76	59	26	62	18	M	T
		3-1		61	63	70	65	9				
52		1-1		48	54	70	57	22	57	22	M	T
56		1-1		48	52	59	53	11	53	11	D	L
		2-2 B		87	89	90	89	3	89	3	E	VL

[126]

Basic Major Tonal Patterns
Subdominant Function

Number	Pattern	Level Test ITML	Item	4-6	7-9	10-12	Comp.	Growth	Diff.	Growth	Diff.	Growth
									Over-all		Category	
1	[music]	1-1	[music]	39	50	61	50	22	50	22	M	T
		1-2 T-B	[music]	80	94	96	90	16	90	16	E	T
3	[music]	1-1	[music]	39	57	72	56	33	69	20	E	T
		4-1	[music]		78	85	82	7				
		1-2 B	[music]	59	67	78	68	19	72	15	VD	L
		4-2 T	[music]		69	80	75	11				
5	[music]	1-1	[music]	39	57	72	56	33	67	18	E	T
		2-1	[music]	48	50	74	57	26				
		4-1	[music]		78	85	82	7				
		4-1	[music]		69	74	72	5				
		1-2 B	[music]	59	67	78	68	19	78	17	D	T
		2-2 T-B	[music]	78	89	91	86	13				
		3-2 B	[music]	70	85	96	84	26				
		4-2 T-B	[music]		69	80	75	11				
		1-3	[music]	56	76	83	72	27	53	37	VD	VH
		4-3	[music]		10	57	34	47				
6	[music]	1-1	[music]	39	52	54	48	15	60	20	M	T
		1-1	[music]	39	50	61	50	22				
		3-1	[music]	52	62	72	62	20				
		4-1	[music]		69	93	81	24				

Number	Level Pattern	Level ITML	Level Item	Difficulty 4-6	7-9	10-12	Comp.	Growth	Over-all Diff.	Over-all Growth	Category Diff.	Category Growth
		1-2 T-B	*(music notation)*	80	89	96	88	16				
		1-2 T	*(music notation)*	76	83	87	82	11				
		1-2 T-B	*(music notation)*	80	94	96	90	16	74	22	D	T
		3-2 T-B	*(music notation)*	37	65	82	61	45				
		4-2 B	*(music notation)*		39	59	49	20				
9	*(music notation)*	2-1	*(music notation)*	48	50	74	57	26	57	26	M	T
		2-2 T-B	*(music notation)*	78	89	91	86	13	85	20	M	T
		3-2 B	*(music notation)*	70	85	96	84	26				
		1-3	*(music notation)*	72	81	92	82	20	82	20	VE	VL
10	*(music notation)*	1-1	*(music notation)*	39	52	54	48	15				
		1-1	*(music notation)*	39	50	61	50	22	51	15	M	L
		1-1	*(music notation)*	52	57	59	56	7				
		1-2 T-B	*(music notation)*	80	89	96	88	16				
		1-2 B	*(music notation)*	80	94	96	90	16	73	24	D	H
		1-2 T-B	*(music notation)*	22	37	63	41	41				
		1-3	*(music notation)*	68	81	90	80	22				
		2-3	*(music notation)*	54	56	69	60	15	68	29	M	T
		4-3	*(music notation)*		39	90	65	51				

Number	Pattern	Level Test ITML	Item	Difficulty 4-6	7-9	10-12	Comp.	Growth	Over-all Diff.	Growth	Category Diff.	Growth
19	[musical notation]	2-1	[musical notation]	48	50	74	57	26	57	26	M	T
		2-2 T-B	[musical notation]	78	89	91	86	13	85	20	M	T
		3-2 B	[musical notation]	70	85	96	84	26				
20	[musical notation]	1-1	[musical notation]	39	52	54	48	15				
		1-1	[musical notation]	39	50	61	50	22	51	15	M	L
		1-1	[musical notation]	52	57	59	56	7				
		1-2 T-B	[musical notation]	80	89	96	88	16	89	16	E	T
		1-2 T-B	[musical notation]	80	94	96	90	16				
23	[musical notation]	1-1	[musical notation]	39	57	72	56	33	69	20	E	T
		4-1	[musical notation]		78	85	82	7				
		1-2 B	[musical notation]	59	67	78	68	19	72	15	VD	L
		4-2 T	[musical notation]		69	80	75	11				
25	[musical notation]	1-1	[musical notation]	23	50	61	45	38	45	38	D	VH
		1-2 T-B	[musical notation]	67	94	96	86	29	86	29	M	VH

[129]

Complex Major Tonal Patterns
Chromaticism

Number	Pattern	Level Test ITML	Item	Difficulty 4-6	7-9	10-12	Comp.	Growth	Over-all Diff.	Growth	Category Diff.	Growth
1		2-1		57	59	62	59	5	59	5	VE	VL
		2-2 T-B		70	83	89	81	19	81	19	M	T
26		2-1		39	48	56	51	17	51	17	D	T
		2-2 T-B		70	91	93	85	23	85	23	M	T
27		2-3		70	75	83	76	13	76	13	M	L
31		2-3		62	78	84	75	22	75	22	M	T
33		2-1		44	55	66	55	22	55	22	M	H
		2-2 B		22	57	63	47	41	47	41	VD	H
34		2-1		43	49	59	50	16	50	16	D	T
		2-2 T-B		83	85	87	85	4	85	4	M	VL
40		2-1		44	55	66	55	22	55	22	M	H
		2-2 T-B		83	85	87	85	4	85	4	M	VL
		2-3		62	78	84	75	22	75	22	M	T

[130]

Number	Pattern	Level Test ITML	Item	Difficulty 4-6	7-9	10-12	Comp.	Growth	Over-all Diff.	Over-all Growth	Category Diff.	Category Growth
		1-2 T	*(musical notation)*	74	93	96	88	22				
		2-2 D	*(musical notation)*	72	83	93	83	21				
		2-2 T	*(musical notation)*	59	76	89	75	30	78	18	D	T
		2-2 B	*(musical notation)*	72	91	96	86	24				
		2-2 T-B	*(musical notation)*	80	82	83	82	3				
		3-2 B	*(musical notation)*	70	85	96	84	26				
		3-2 T	*(musical notation)*	70	72	91	78	21				
		3-2 B	*(musical notation)*	69	80	87	79	18				
		4-2 B	*(musical notation)*		85	91	88	6				
		4-2 T	*(musical notation)*		65	82	74	17				
		4-2 T-B	*(musical notation)*		69	80	74	11				
		4-2 T	*(musical notation)*		39	59	49	20				
		1-3	*(musical notation)*	69	81	89	80	20				
		2-3	*(musical notation)*	62	78	84	75	22				
		3-3	*(musical notation)*	80	83	97	87	17	70	29	M	T
		3-3	*(musical notation)*	71	83	88	81	17				
		4-3	*(musical notation)*		39	90	65	51				
		4-3	*(musical notation)*		10	57	34	47				
2	*(musical notation)*	1-1	*(musical notation)*	48	57	67	57	19				
		1-1	*(musical notation)*	37	61	63	54	26				
		1-1	*(musical notation)*	52	57	59	56	7				
		2-1	*(musical notation)*	63	65	67	65	4				

Number	Pattern	Level / Test / ITML	Item	Difficulty 4-6	7-9	10-12	Comp.	Growth	Over-all Diff.	Over-all Growth	Category Diff.	Category Growth
		2-1	*(music notation)*	57	59	62	59	5	67	13	M	T
		3-1	*(music notation)*	69	87	96	84	27				
		4-1	*(music notation)*		70	85	78	15				
		4-1	*(music notation)*		69	74	72	5				
		4-1	*(music notation)*		69	80	74	11				
		1-2 T	*(music notation)*	59	67	78	68	19				
		1-2 B	*(music notation)*	44	72	74	63	30				
		1-2 B	*(music notation)*	74	93	96	88	22				
		2-2 T	*(music notation)*	70	72	96	79	26				
		2-2 B	*(music notation)*	59	76	89	75	30				
		2-2 T	*(music notation)*	72	91	96	86	24				
		3-2 B	*(music notation)*	70	83	94	82	24	75	22	VD	T
		3-2 T	*(music notation)*	70	85	96	84	26				
		3-2 T	*(music notation)*	37	65	82	61	45				
		3-2 T-B	*(music notation)*	82	84	88	85	6				
		4-2 T-B	*(music notation)*		78	93	86	13				
		4-2 T-B	*(music notation)*		65	82	74	17				
		4-2 T-B	*(music notation)*		35	43	39	8				
		2-3	*(music notation)*	55	59	73	62	18				
		2-3	*(music notation)*	70	75	83	76	13	68	23	M	T
		4-3	*(music notation)*		43	83	63	40				

[132]

Number	Pattern	Level Test ITML	Item	4-6	7-9	10-12	Comp.	Growth	Over-all Diff.	Over-all Growth	Category Diff.	Category Growth
3	🎼	3-1	🎼	67	78	87	77	20				
		4-1	🎼		76	91	84	15	80	18	M	T
		2-2 T	🎼	72	91	96	86	24				
		3-2 T	🎼	70	72	91	78	21				
		3-2 T-B	🎼	82	84	88	85	6	84	13	M	T
		4-2 T-B	🎼		85	87	86	2				
4	🎼	1-1	🎼	78	85	89	84	11				
		1-1	🎼	39	57	72	56	33				
		1-1	🎼	43	80	82	68	39				
		1-1	🎼	48	52	59	53	11				
		2-1	🎼	50	52	76	59	26				
		2-1	🎼	44	59	87	63	43	69	23	M	H
		3-1	🎼	69	87	96	84	27				
		3-1	🎼	61	63	70	65	9				
		3-1	🎼	67	78	87	77	20				
		4-1	🎼		78	85	82	7				
		1-2 B	🎼	67	96	98	87	31				
		1-2 B	🎼	59	67	78	68	19				
		1-2 T	🎼	22	37	63	41	41				
		1-2 T-B	🎼	74	87	91	84	17				
		1-2 T	🎼	61	85	87	78	26				

[133]

Number	Pattern	Level Test ITML	Item	Difficulty 4-6	7-9	10-12	Comp.	Growth	Over-all Diff.	Over-all Growth	Category Diff.	Category Growth
		1-2 T-B	(musical notation)	87	89	90	89	3				
		1-2 T	(musical notation)	74	93	96	88	22				
		2-2 B	(musical notation)	72	83	93	83	21	79	21	D	T
		2-2 B	(musical notation)	72	91	96	86	24				
		3-2 B	(musical notation)	70	83	94	82	24				
		3-2 B	(musical notation)	70	85	96	84	26				
		3-2 T	(musical notation)	70	72	91	78	21				
		3-2 B	(musical notation)	57	72	87	72	30				
		4-2 T	(musical notation)		82	83	83	1				
		4-2 T-B	(musical notation)		69	80	75	11				
		1-3	(musical notation)	69	81	89	80	20				
		2-3	(musical notation)	62	78	84	75	22	81	18	M	T
		3-3	(musical notation)	80	83	97	89	11				
		3-3	(musical notation)	71	83	88	81	17				
5	(musical notation)	4-1	(musical notation)		76	91	84	15	84	15	E	T
		4-2 T-B	(musical notation)		85	87	86	2	86	2	E	VL
6	(musical notation)	1-1	(musical notation)	78	85	89	84	11				
		1-1	(musical notation)	43	80	82	68	39				
		1-1	(musical notation)	48	52	59	53	11	72	22	M	T
		3-1	(musical notation)	69	87	96	84	27				
		1-2 B	(musical notation)	67	96	98	87	31				

Number	Pattern	ITML	Item	4-6	7-9	10-12	Comp.	Growth	Diff.	Growth	Diff.	Growth
						Difficulty			Over-all		Category	
		1-2 T-B		74	87	91	87	17				
		1-2 T-B		87	89	90	89	3	86	19	E	T
		3-2 B		70	83	94	82	24				
		1-3		68	81	89	80	20				
		3-3		70	91	80	21	75	31	M	T	
		3-3		39	90	64	51					
7		4-1		76	91	84	15	84	15	E	T	
		4-2 T-B		85	87	86	2	86	2	E	VI	
		1-3		72	81	92	82	20	82	20	M	T
8		1-1		78	85	89	84	11				
		1-1		43	80	82	68	39	68	20	M	T
		1-1		48	52	59	53	11				
		1-2 B		67	96	98	87	31				
		1-2 T-B		74	87	91	84	17				
		1-2 T-B		87	89	90	89	3	86	19	E	T
		3-2 B		70	83	94	82	24				
		1-3		69	81	89	80	20				
		1-3		68	81	90	80	22				
		3-3		80	83	97	87	17	78	28	M	T
		4-3		39	90	65	51					

[135]

Number	Pattern	ITML	Item	Difficulty 4-6	7-9	10-12	Comp.	Growth	Over-all Diff.	Growth	Category Diff.	Growth
9	♪	1-1	♪	52	57	59	56	7	56	7	D	L
		1-3	♪	72	81	92	82	20	82	20	M	T
10	♪	1-3	♪	61	81	89	80	20				
		1-3	♪	68	81	90	80	22	78	21	M	T
		2-3	♪	62	78	84	75	22				
11	♪	1-1	♪	48	57	67	57	19				
		1-1	♪	52	57	59	56	7				
		2-1	♪	63	65	67	64	4	62	8	D	L
		2-1	♪	57	59	62	59	5				
		4-1	♪		69	74	72	5				
		1-2 B	♪	74	93	96	88	22				
		2-2 B	♪	70	72	96	79	26				
		2-2 B	♪	59	76	89	75	30				
		2-2 T	♪	72	91	96	86	24	83	21	M	T
		3-2 T	♪	70	85	96	84	26				
		3-2 T-B	♪	82	84	88	85	6				
		4-2 B	♪		78	93	86	15				
		2-3	♪	70	75	83	76	13	76	13	M	L
12	♪	1-1	♪	48	57	67	57	19	57	19	D	T
		1-2 T-B	♪	74	93	96	88	22				
		2-2 T	♪	70	72	96	79	26	71	30	VD	H

Number	Pattern	Level Test ITML	Item	4-6	7-9	10-12	Comp.	Growth	Over-all Diff.	Over-all Growth	Category Diff.	Category Growth
		2-2 T	*(musical notation)*	22	57	63	47	41				
		4-3	*(musical notation)*		43	83	63	40	63	40	D	H
13	*(musical notation)*	1-1	*(musical notation)*	48	57	67	57	19				
		1-1	*(musical notation)*	52	57	59	56	7				
		2-1	*(musical notation)*	63	65	67	65	4	61	8	D	L
		2-1	*(musical notation)*	57	59	62	53	5				
		4-1	*(musical notation)*		69	74	72	5				
		1-2 B	*(musical notation)*	74	93	96	88	22				
		2-2 T-B	*(musical notation)*	59	76	89	75	30				
		2-2 T-B	*(musical notation)*	72	91	96	86	24				
		3-2 T	*(musical notation)*	70	85	96	84	26	84	21	M	T
		3-2 T-B	*(musical notation)*	82	84	88	85	6				
		4-2 B	*(musical notation)*		78	93	86	15				
		2-3	*(musical notation)*	70	75	83	76	13	76	13	M	L
14	*(musical notation)*	1-1	*(musical notation)*	48	57	67	57	19	57	19	D	T
		1-2 T-B	*(musical notation)*	74	93	96	88	22	88	22	VE	T
		4-3	*(musical notation)*		43	83	63	40	63	40	D	H
15	*(musical notation)*	4-1	*(musical notation)*		70	82	76	12	76	12	M	T
		2-2 T	*(musical notation)*	59	76	89	75	30	82	18	M	T
		4-2 T	*(musical notation)*		85	91	88	6				

[137]

Number	Level			Difficulty					Over-all		Category	
	Pattern	Test (ITML)	Item	4-6	7-9	10-12	Comp.	Growth	Diff.	Growth	Diff.	Growth
16	[music]	3-1	[music]	69	87	96	84	27	84	27	E	H
17	[music]	4-1	[music]		70	82	76	12	76	12	M	T
		4-2 T	[music]		78	93	86	15	87	10	VE	T
		4-2 T-B	[music]		85	91	88	6				
18	[music]	3-2 T	[music]	70	72	91	78	21	78	21	D	T
19	[music]	1-2 T	[music]	61	85	87	78	26	78	24	D	T
		3-2 T	[music]	70	72	91	78	21				
22	[music]	1-3	[music]	72	81	92	82	20	82	20	M	T
23	[music]	1-1	[music]	39	52	54	48	15	48	15	VD	T
		1-2 T-B	[music]	80	89	96	88	16	88	16	VE	T
		3-3	[music]	80	83	97	87	17	87	17	E	T
24	[music]	2-3	[music]	62	78	84	75	22	75	22	M	T
25	[music]	1-3	[music]	69	81	89	80	20	58	16	VD	T
		4-3	[music]		30	41	36	11				
26	[music]	1-1	[music]	48	57	67	57	19	64	12	M	T
		4-1	[music]		69	74	72	5				
		1-2 B	[music]	74	93	96	88	22	60	24	VD	T
		2-2 T	[music]	70	72	96	32	26				
30	[music]	4-1	[music]		70	85	78	15	78	15	M	T

Number	Pattern	ITML	Item	4-6	7-9	10-12	Comp.	Growth	Over-all Diff.	Over-all Growth	Category Diff.	Category Growth
		3-2 B		70	83	94	82	24	84	20	M	T
		4-2 T-B			78	93	86	15				
31		1-1		48	57	67	57	19				
		1-1		52	57	59	56	7				
		2-1		63	65	67	65	4	62	8	D	L
		2-1		57	59	62	59	5				
		4-1			69	74	72	5				
		1-2 B		74	93	96	88	22				
		2-2 T		70	72	96	79	26				
		2-2 B		59	76	89	75	30				
		2-2 T		72	91	96	86	24	83	21	M	T
		3-2 T		70	85	96	84	26				
		3-2 T-B		82	84	88	85	6				
		4-2 B			78	93	86	15				
		2-3		70	75	83	76	13	76	13	M	L
32		1-1		48	57	67	57	19	57	19	D	T
		1-2 T-B		74	93	96	88	22	84	24	M	T
		2-2 T		70	72	96	79	26				
		4-3			43	83	63	40	63	40	D	H
33		4-1			76	91	84	15	84	15	E	T
		4-2 T-B			85	87	86	2	86	2	E	VL

Number	Pattern	ITML	Item	4-6	7-9	10-12	Comp.	Growth	Diff.	Growth	Diff.	Growth
34	♪(notation)	1-1	♪(notation)	78	85	89	84	11				
		1-1	♪(notation)	43	80	82	68	39	72	22	M	T
		1-1	♪(notation)	48	52	59	53	11				
		3-1	♪(notation)	69	87	96	84	27				
		1-2 B	♪(notation)	67	96	98	87	22				
		1-2 B	♪(notation)	78	87	91	84	27	86	19	E	T
		1-2 T-B	♪(notation)	87	89	90	89	3				
		3-2 B	♪(notation)	70	83	94	82	24				
		1-3	♪(notation)	69	81	89	80	20				
		3-3	♪(notation)	80	83	97	87	17	77	29	M	T
		4-3	♪(notation)		39	90	65	51				
35	♪(notation)	4-1	♪(notation)		76	91	84	15	84	15	E	T
		4-2 T-B	♪(notation)		85	87	86	2	86	2	E	VL
36	♪(notation)	1-1	♪(notation)	78	85	89	84	11				
		1-1	♪(notation)	43	80	82	68	39	72	22	M	T
		1-1	♪(notation)	48	52	59	53	11				
		3-1	♪(notation)	69	87	96	84	27				
		1-2 B	♪(notation)	67	96	98	87	22				
		1-2 B	♪(notation)	74	87	91	84	27	86	19	E	T
		1-2 T-B	♪(notation)	87	89	90	89	3				
		3-2 B	♪(notation)	70	83	94	82	24				

Number	Pattern	Test ITML	Item	4-6	7-9	10-12	Comp.	Growth	Diff.	Growth	Diff.	Growth
									Over-all		Category	
		1-3	[music notation]	69	81	89	80	20				
		3-3	[music notation]	80	83	97	87	17	83	18	E	T
		3-3	[music notation]	71	83	88	81	17				
37	[music notation]	4-1	[music notation]		76	91	84	15	84	15	E	T
		4-2 T-B	[music notation]		85	87	86	2	86	2	E	VL
38	[music notation]	1-1	[music notation]	78	85	89	84	11				
		1-1	[music notation]	43	80	82	68	39	72	22	M	T
		1-1	[music notation]	48	52	59	53	11				
		3-1	[music notation]	69	87	96	84	27				
		1-2 B	[music notation]	67	96	98	87	22				
		1-2 T-B	[music notation]	74	87	91	84	27	86	19	E	T
		1-2 T-B	[music notation]	87	89	90	89	3				
		3-2 B	[music notation]	70	83	94	82	24				
		1-3	[music notation]	69	81	89	80	20	84	18	E	T
		3-3	[music notation]	80	83	97	87	17				
41	[music notation]	1-1	[music notation]	52	57	59	56	7	56	7	D	L

Complex Major Tonal Patterns
Expanded Harmonic Functions

Number	Pattern	ITML (Level Test)	Item	4-6	7-9	10-12	Comp.	Growth	Over-all Diff.	Over-all Growth	Category Diff.	Category Growth
1	*(music)*	2-1	*(music)*	48	50	74	57	26				
		4-1	*(music)*		69	74	72	5	64	16	M	T
		2-2 T-B	*(music)*	78	89	91	86	13				
		2-2 T	*(music)*	59	76	89	75	30	82	20	M	T
		4-2 B	*(music)*		78	93	86	15				
		4-3	*(music)*		10	57	34	47	34	47	D	H
2	*(music)*	2-1	*(music)*	63	65	67	65	4				
		4-1	*(music)*		69	93	81	24	73	14	E	L
		1-2 T	*(music)*	76	83	87	82	11				
		2-2 B	*(music)*	59	76	89	75	30	69	20	M	T
		4-2 B	*(music)*		39	59	49	20				
7	*(music)*	2-1	*(music)*	48	63	76	62	28	62	28	M	H
		2-2 B	*(music)*	70	72	96	79	26				
		2-2 B	*(music)*	80	82	83	82	3	80	15	M	T
8	*(music)*	4-1	*(music)*		69	93	81	24	81	24	VE	T
		2-2 B	*(music)*	80	82	83	82	3				
		4-2 T-B	*(music)*		39	59	49	20	66	12	M	L
13	*(music)*	1-3	*(music)*	72	81	92	82	20	82	20	M	T
18	*(music)*	1-2 B	*(music)*	22	37	63	39	41	39	41	VD	VH

Number	Pattern	Level Test ITML	Item	Difficulty 4-6	7-9	10-12	Comp.	Growth	Over-all Diff.	Growth	Category Diff.	Growth
19	♪	2-1	♪	50	52	76	59	26	62	18	M	T
		3-1	♪	61	63	70	65	9				
		2-2 B	♪	72	83	93	83	21	81	30	M	T
		3-2 T-B	♪	59	80	97	79	38				
		3-3	♪	80	83	97	87	17	87	17	E	T
20	♪	1-1	♪	48	54	70	57	22	65	26	M	T
		2-1	♪	44	59	87	63	43				
		4-1	♪		70	82	76	12				
		1-2 B	♪	61	85	87	78	26	82	25	M	T
		2-2 B	♪	72	91	96	86	24				
21	♪	2-3	♪	55	59	73	62	18	62	18	M	T

Basic Minor Tonal Patterns
Tonic Function

Number	Level			Difficulty					Over-all		Category	
	Pattern	Test ITML	Item	4-6	7-9	10-12	Comp.	Growth	Diff.	Growth	Diff.	Growth
1	(notation)	2-1	(notation)	41	43	69	51	28	51	28	M	H
		2-2 T	(notation)	74	82	93	86	19	86	19	E	T
		3-3	(notation)	66	72	84	74	18	74	16	M	T
		3-3	(notation)	68	76	82	75	14				
2	(notation)	3-3	(notation)	68	76	82	75	14	75	14	M	T
3	(notation)	1-1	(notation)	44	59	65	56	21	56	21	M	T
		1-2 T-B	(notation)	59	76	87	74	28	81	21	M	T
		1-2 B	(notation)	83	91	94	89	11				
		1-2 B	(notation)	72	78	91	80	19				
		2-2 T	(notation)	69	82	93	81	24				
		2-3	(notation)	66	76	83	75	17	65	24	M	T
		2-3	(notation)	57	68	75	67	18				
		4-3	(notation)		34	71	52	37				
4	(notation)	1-1	(notation)	44	59	65	56	21	54	14	M	T
		3-1	(notation)	50	52	58	53	8				
		1-2 B	(notation)	83	92	94	89	11	79	21	M	T
		1-2 B	(notation)	72	78	91	80	19				
		2-2 T	(notation)	69	82	93	81	24				
		3-2 B	(notation)	48	67	87	67	29				

[144]

Number	Pattern	Level Test ITML	Item	Difficulty					Over-all		Category	
				4-6	7-9	10-12	Comp.	Growth	Diff.	Growth	Diff.	Growth
		1-3		58	73	79	70	11				
		2-3		57	68	76	67	18	57	13	D	L
		4-3			30	40	35	10				
5		1-1		80	89	94	88	14				
		2-1		39	57	59	52	20				
		2-1		52	69	72	64	20	62	17	M	T
		2-1		48	52	72	57	24				
		4-1			46	52	49	6				
		1-2 T		59	76	87	74	18				
		1-2 T-B		72	87	89	83	17				
		2-2 T		65	82	96	81	31				
		2-2 T-B		63	74	89	75	26	76	19	M	T
		2-2 T-B		37	50	70	52	33				
		2-2 T-B		70	72	89	77	19				
		3-2 B		78	83	87	83	9				
		4-2 T			80	82	81	2				
		2-3		61	77	79	72	18	74	16	M	T
		3-3		68	76	82	75	14				
6		1-1		43	52	56	50	13				

[145]

Number	Pattern	Level Test ITML	Item	Difficulty 4-6	7-9	10-12	Comp.	Growth	Over-all Diff.	Growth	Category Diff.	Growth
		1-1		39	43	61	48	22				
		2-1		48	54	78	60	30				
		2-1		41	43	69	51	28	57	23	M	T
		3-1		54	65	78	66	24				
		4-1			54	74	64	20				
		1-2 T-B		59	76	87	74	28				
		1-2 T		76	83	93	84	17				
		1-2 T		72	78	91	80	19				
		1-2 T-B		72	91	96	86	24	76	27	M	T
		2-2 T-B		44	69	76	63	32				
		3-2 T-B		48	83	87	73	39				
		3-2 T-B		57	70	87	71	30				
		2-3		54	56	69	60	15				
		3-3		66	72	84	74	18	56	14	D	T
		4-3			30	40	35	10				
8		4-1			61	69	65	8	65	8	E	L
		1-2 B		59	76	87	74	28	74	28	M	H
9		1-1		80	87	94	87	14				
		1-1		43	52	56	50	13				

[146]

Number	Pattern	Level Test ITML	Item	4-6	7-9	10-12	Comp.	Growth	Diff.	Growth	Diff.	Growth
		2-1		39	57	59	52	20	59	17	M	T
		2-1		52	69	72	64	20				
		2-1		41	43	69	51	28				
		3-1		48	50	57	52	9				
		1-2 B		59	76	87	74	28	67	24	D	T
		2-2 T		65	82	96	81	31				
		2-2 T-B		63	74	89	75	26				
		2-2 B		70	72	89	77	18				
		2-2 T		57	74	87	73	30				
		3-2 T-B		13	19	26	19	13				
		2-3		66	76	83	75	17	74	16	M	T
		2-3		61	77	79	72	18				
		3-3		68	76	82	75	14				
10		1-1		50	54	61	55	11				
		1-1		43	52	56	50	13				
		1-1		46	57	67	57	21				
		1-1		44	59	70	58	26				
		2-1		63	72	89	75	26				
		2-1		41	43	69	51	28	59	18	M	T

Number	Pattern	Level Test ITML	Item	4-6	7-9	10-12	Comp.	Growth	Diff.	Growth	Diff.	Growth
		3-1	*[musical notation]*	50	52	58	53	8				
		3-1	*[musical notation]*	50	58	65	58	15				
		3-1	*[musical notation]*	61	67	74	67	13				
		3-1	*[musical notation]*	54	58	63	58	9				
		3-1	*[musical notation]*	54	69	78	67	24				
		1-2 B	*[musical notation]*	83	91	94	89	11				
		1-2 B	*[musical notation]*	59	76	87	74	28				
		1-2 B	*[musical notation]*	72	87	89	83	17				
		1-2 T	*[musical notation]*	70	82	89	80	19				
		1-2 T	*[musical notation]*	76	83	93	84	17				
		1-2 T	*[musical notation]*	72	78	91	80	19				
		1-2 T	*[musical notation]*	72	91	96	86	24	78	21	M	T
		2-2 B	*[musical notation]*	72	83	96	84	24				
		2-2 B	*[musical notation]*	37	52	74	54	37				
		2-2 T	*[musical notation]*	70	72	89	77	19				
		3-2 T-B	*[musical notation]*	57	72	87	72	30				
		3-2 T-B	*[musical notation]*	57	70	87	71	30				
		4-2 B	*[musical notation]*		82	83	82	1				
		3-3	*[musical notation]*	66	72	84	74	18	74	18	M	T

Number	Level Test			Difficulty					Over-all		Category	
	Pattern	ITML	Item	4-6	7-9	10-12	Comp.	Growth	Diff.	Growth	Diff.	Growth
11		2-1		54	56	64	58	10	54	19	M	T
		2-1		41	43	69	51	28				
		2-2 B		57	74	87	73	30	73	30	M	H
		2-3		57	68	77	67	20	67	20	M	T
13		4-1			61	69	65	8	65	8	E	L
		2-3		57	68	77	67	20	51	30	D	VH
		4-3			30	40	35	10				
14		2-1		41	43	69	51	28	51	28	M	H
		2-2 T-B		74	82	93	83	19	83	19	M	T
16		2-1		59	76	87	71	28	71	28	VE	H
19		1-1		80	87	94	87	14	61	18	M	T
		2-1		39	57	59	52	20				
		2-1		52	69	72	43	20				
		2-2 T-B		63	74	89	75	26	76	23	M	T
		2-2 T-B		70	72	89	77	19				
20		1-1		46	57	59	54	13	57	21	M	T
		2-1		41	43	69	51	28				
		3-1		54	65	76	65	22				

[149]

Number	Pattern	Level Test ITML	Item	4-6	7-9	10-12	Comp.	Growth	Over-all Diff.	Over-all Growth	Category Diff.	Category Growth
		1-2 B		59	76	87	71	28				
		1-2 T		76	83	93	84	17	78	25	M	T
		1-2 T-B		72	91	96	86	24				
		3-2 T-B		57	70	87	71	30				
		3-3		66	72	84	74	18	74	18	M	T
21		1-1		43	52	56	50	13	50	13	D	T
		2-2 T		69	82	93	81	24	81	24	M	T
		2-3		66	76	83	75	17	75	17	M	T
22		1-1		44	59	65	56	21	54	14	M	T
		3-1		50	52	58	53	8				
		1-2 T-B		72	78	91	80	19	84	15	E	L
		1-2 B		83	91	94	89	11				
23		1-2 T		59	76	87	74	28	74	28	M	H
24		1-2 T		72	78	91	80	19	80	19	M	T
30		2-3		54	56	69	60	15	60	15	D	T
31		1-1		43	52	56	50	13	50	13	D	T
		1-2 B		59	76	87	74	28	74	28	VD	H

Number	Level			Difficulty					Over-all		Category	
	Pattern	ITML	Item	4-6	7-9	10-12	Comp.	Growth	Diff.	Growth	Diff.	Growth
33	𝄞♪	1-1	𝄞♪	43	52	56	50	13	50	13	D	T
37	𝄞♪	3-3	𝄞♪	68	76	82	75	14	75	14	M	T
38	𝄞♪	4-1	𝄞♪		61	69	65	8	65	8	E	L
41	𝄞♪	2-1	𝄞♪	41	43	69	51	28	51	28	M	H
43	𝄞♪	4-1	𝄞♪		54	74	64	20	64	20	E	T
		1-2 T	𝄞♪	59	76	82	56	28	56	28	VD	H
44	𝄞♪	1-1	𝄞♪	43	52	56	47	13	49	20	D	T
		2-1	𝄞♪	41	43	69	51	28				
		1-2 T-B	𝄞♪	59	76	87	74	28	74	28	M	H
45	𝄞♪	1-1	𝄞♪	44	59	65	56	21	56	21	M	T
		1-2 B	𝄞♪	83	91	94	89	11	84	15	E	L
		1-2 B	𝄞♪	72	78	91	80	19				

Number	Pattern	Level Test ITML	Item	Difficulty 4-6	7-9	10-12	Comp.	Growth	Over-all Diff.	Growth	Category Diff.	Growth
3	(notation)	1-1	(notation)	37	46	54	46	17	46	20	D	T
		2-1	(notation)	32	52	56	47	24				
		1-2 T-B	(notation)	56	69	72	86	16	86	16	E	T
4	(notation)	3-2 T	(notation)	57	72	87	72	30	72	30	M	T
5	(notation)	2-1	(notation)	52	69	72	64	20	60	22	E	H
		2-1	(notation)	48	52	72	57	24				
		2-2 T-B	(notation)	37	50	70	52	33	52	33	VD	H
6	(notation)	2-1	(notation)	541	56	64	55	10	55	10	M	L
		2-2 B	(notation)	57	74	87	73	30	73	30	M	T
9	(notation)	1-1	(notation)	37	46	54	46	17	55	24	M	H
		1-1	(notation)	31	48	50	43	19				
		2-1	(notation)	50	79	85	70	35				
		2-1	(notation)	31	62	67	53	36				
		3-1	(notation)	58	63	69	63	11				
		1-2 T-B	(notation)	78	87	89	85	11	77	21	M	T
		1-2 B	(notation)	72	78	91	80	19				
		2-2 T-B	(notation)	67	74	98	80	31				
		2-2 T-B	(notation)	65	82	96	81	31				
		2-2 T-B	(notation)	37	52	74	54	37				
		3-2 T-B	(notation)	69	80	89	79	20				
		4-2 T-B	(notation)		82	83	82	1				

Number	Pattern	Test ITML	Item	4-6	7-9	10-12	Comp.	Growth	Over-all Diff.	Over-all Growth	Category Diff.	Category Growth
		1-3	♪	77	87	93	86	16	84	20	M	H
		3-3	♪	69	80	93	81	24				
10	♪	1-1	♪	31	48	50	43	19				
		1-1	♪	44	59	65	56	21				
		2-1	♪	54	56	64	58	10	57	16	M	T
		4-1	♪		54	74	64	20				
		4-1	♪		61	69	65	8				
		1-2 B	♪	83	91	94	89	11				
		1-2 T-B	♪	44	72	74	63	30				
		1-2 T	♪	72	78	91	80	19	74	27	M	T
		2-2 B	♪	57	74	87	73	30				
		3-2 B	♪	48	67	87	67	39				
		3-2 T-B	♪	57	72	87	72	30				
		2-3	♪	57	68	75	67	18	67	18	D	T
13	♪	2-2 T-B	♪	74	82	93	83	19	83	19	E	T
19	♪	1-2 T	♪	76	83	93	84	16	83	8	E	L
		4-2 T	♪		82	83	82	1				
23	♪	2-1	♪	54	56	64	58	10	58	10	M	L
		2-2 B	♪	57	74	87	73	30	73	30	M	T

Number	Level			Difficulty					Over-all		Category	
	Test			4-6	7-9	10-12	Comp.	Growth	Diff.	Growth	Diff.	Growth
	Pattern	ITML	Item									
24		1-2 T-B		78	87	89	85	11	85	11	E	L
34		3-3		68	76	82	75	14	75	14	M	L
48		1-1		31	48	50	40	19	40	19	VD	T
50		2-1		54	56	64	58	10	58	10	M	L
		2-2 B		57	74	87	73	30	73	30	M	T
51		2-1		46	48	67	54	21	56	15	M	T
		3-1		54	58	63	58	9				
		2-2 T-B		37	52	74	54	37				
		3-2 T-B		69	80	89	79	20	72	19	M	T
		4-2 T-B			82	83	82	1				
52		2-3		57	68	75	87	18	87	18	E	T

Basic Minor Tonal Patterns
Subdominant Function

Number	Pattern	Level Test ITML	Item	4-6	7-9	10-12	Comp.	Growth	Diff. (Over-all)	Growth (Over-all)	Diff. (Category)	Growth (Category)
1	[notation]	1-1	[notation]	46	57	59	51	13	51	13	M	T
		1-2 T-B	[notation]	72	91	96	86	24	86	24	E	T
3	[notation]	1-1	[notation]	50	54	61	55	11	55	11	M	L
		1-2 B	[notation]	70	82	89	80	19	82	11	M	VL
		4-2 T	[notation]		82	85	84	3				
5	[notation]	1-1	[notation]	50	54	61	55	11				
		2-1	[notation]	44	62	67	58	23	50	15	D	T
		4-1	[notation]		32	43	38	11				
		1-2 T-B	[notation]	70	82	89	80	19				
		2-2 T-B	[notation]	67	74	98	80	31				
		2-2 T	[notation]	72	83	93	83	21	79	23	M	T
		3-2 B	[notation]	48	67	87	67	39				
		4-2 B	[notation]		82	85	84	3				
6	[notation]	1-1	[notation]	48	56	61	55	13				
		1-1	[notation]	39	43	61	48	22				
		1-1	[notation]	46	57	59	54	13	51	18	M	T
		2-1	[notation]	32	52	56	47	24				
		1-2 B	[notation]	76	83	87	82	11				
		1-2 T-B	[notation]	76	83	93	84	16				

[155]

Number	Pattern	ITML (Level Test)	Item	4-6	7-9	10-12	Comp.	Growth	Over-all Diff.	Over-all Growth	Category Diff.	Category Growth
		1-2 T-B	*(musical notation)*	72	91	96	86	24	81	20	M	T
		3-2 B	*(musical notation)*	57	72	87	72	30				
9	*(musical notation)*	2-1	*(musical notation)*	44	62	67	58	23	58	23	E	H
		2-2 T-B	*(musical notation)*	67	74	98	80	31				
		2-2 T-B	*(musical notation)*	65	82	96	81	31	78	27	M	T
		3-2 B	*(musical notation)*	46	67	87	67	41				
		4-2 T-B	*(musical notation)*		82	85	84	3				
		3-3	*(musical notation)*	69	80	82	77	13	77	13	E	L
10	*(musical notation)*	1-1	*(musical notation)*	37	56	61	51	24				
		1-1	*(musical notation)*	39	43	61	48	22	53	22	M	H
		1-1	*(musical notation)*	46	57	59	54	13				
		2-1	*(musical notation)*	48	54	78	60	30				
		1-2 B	*(musical notation)*	76	83	87	82	11				
		1-2 B	*(musical notation)*	76	83	93	84	17				
		1-2 T-B	*(musical notation)*	72	91	96	86	24	79	21	M	T
		2-2 T-B	*(musical notation)*	44	69	76	63	32				
		2-3	*(musical notation)*	57	68	77	67	20	60	29	D	H
		4-3	*(musical notation)*		34	71	53	37				
17	*(musical notation)*	2-2 T	*(musical notation)*	37	50	70	52	33	52	33	VD	VH

[156]

Number	Level Pattern	Level Test ITML	Item	4-6	7-9	10-12	Comp.	Growth	Diff.	Growth	Diff.	Growth
19	(staff)	2-2 T-B	(staff)	67	74	98	80	31				
		3-2 B	(staff)	48	67	87	67	39	77	24	M	T
		4-2 T-B	(staff)		82	85	84	3				
20	(staff)	1-1	(staff)	37	56	61	51	24				
		1-1	(staff)	39	43	61	48	22	51	20	M	T
		1-1	(staff)	46	57	59	54	13				
		1-2 B	(staff)	76	83	87	82	11				
		1-2 B	(staff)	76	83	93	84	17	84	17	M	T
		1-2 T-B	(staff)	72	91	96	86	24				
23	(staff)	1-1	(staff)	50	54	61	55	11	55	11	M	L
		1-2 T-B	(staff)	70	82	89	80	19	80	19	M	T
25	(staff)	1-1	(staff)	46	57	59	54	13	54	13	M	T
		1-2 T	(staff)	72	91	96	86	24	86	24	E	T

Complex Minor Tonal Patterns
Chromaticism

Number	Pattern	Level Test ITML	Item	Difficulty 4-6	7-9	10-12	Comp.	Growth	Over-all Diff.	Growth	Category Diff.	Growth
17		2-2 T-B		72	83	96	84	24	84	24	E	T
21		2-3		57	68	75	67	18	67	18	M	T
23		2-1		48	52	72	57	24	57	24	M	H
		2-2 T-B		37	50	70	52	33	52	33	D	H
25		2-2 T-B		63	74	89	75	26	78	27	M	T
		3-2 T		65	82	93	80	28				
27		2-3		61	77	79	72	18	72	18	M	T
41		2-1		52	69	72	64	20	64	20	E	T
		2-3		54	56	69	60	15	60	15	D	L
44		1-1		39	57	59	52	20	52	20	D	T
45		2-2 T-B		70	72	89	77	19	77	19	M	L
		2-3		66	76	83	75	17	75	17	E	T

[158]

Complex Minor Tonal Patterns
Combined Harmonic Functions

Number	Pattern	Test ITML	Item	4-6	7-9	10-12	Comp.	Growth	Diff.	Growth	Diff.	Growth
1	♪	1-1	♪	80	87	94	87	14				
		1-1	♪	37	46	54	45	17				
		1-1	♪	50	54	61	55	11				
		1-1	♪	56	69	72	66	16				
		1-1	♪	31	48	50	43	19				
		1-1	♪	48	56	61	55	13				
		2-1	♪	52	74	85	70	33	59	17	M	T
		2-1	♪	46	48	67	54	21				
		2-1	♪	44	62	67	58	23				
		2-1	♪	54	56	64	58	10				
		2-1	♪	63	72	89	75	26				
		3-1	♪	50	58	65	58	15				
		3-1	♪	54	58	63	58	9				
		4-1	♪		32	43	38	11				
		1-2 T	♪	83	91	94	89	11				
		1-2 T-B	♪	78	87	89	85	11				
		1-2 T-B	♪	72	82	89	81	17				
		1-2 T-B	♪	70	82	89	80	19				
		1-2 B	♪	76	83	87	82	13				
		1-2 T-B	♪	83	89	94	89	11				

Number	Pattern	Level Test ITML	Item	Difficulty 4-6	7-9	10-12	Comp.	Growth	Over-all Diff.	Over-all Growth	Category Diff.	Category Growth
		1-2 .B	(music notation)	76	83	93	84	17				
		2-2 T-B	(music notation)	67	74	98	80	31	82	17	M	T
		2-2 T-B	(music notation)	65	82	96	81	31				
		2-2 T-B	(music notation)	72	83	96	84	24				
		2-2 T-B	(music notation)	72	83	93	83	21				
		2-2 T-B	(music notation)	74	82	93	83	19				
		2-2 T-B	(music notation)	57	74	87	73	30				
		3-2 T-B	(music notation)	69	80	89	79	20				
		4-2 T-B	(music notation)		82	85	84	3				
		4-2 B	(music notation)		82	83	82	1				
		1-3	(music notation)	72	80	93	82	21				
		1-3	(music notation)	77	87	93	86	16	82	18	M	T
		3-3	(music notation)	69	80	82	77	13				
		4-3	(music notation)		70	91	81	21				
2	(music notation)	1-1	(music notation)	68	82	93	81	25				
		1-1	(music notation)	44	59	65	56	21				
		2-1	(music notation)	32	52	56	47	24				
		2-1	(music notation)	59	69	72	67	13				
		2-1	(music notation)	48	54	78	60	30				
		2-1	(music notation)	48	54	72	57	24				
		3-1	(music notation)	50	52	58	53	8	59	17	M	T
		3-1	(music notation)	61	67	74	67	13				
		3-1	(music notation)	54	65	78	66	24				

Number	Pattern	Level Test ITML	Item	4-6	7-9	10-12	Comp.	Growth	Diff.	Growth	Diff.	Growth
									Over-all		Category	
		3-1	(musical notation)	48	50	57	52	9				
		4-1	(musical notation)		32	43	38	11				
		4-1	(musical notation)		46	52	49	6				
		4-1	(musical notation)	54	74	64	20					
		4-1	(musical notation)		61	69	65	8				
		1-2 T-B	(musical notation)	83	91	94	89	11				
		1-2 T-B	(musical notation)	72	96	98	89	26				
		1-2 T	(musical notation)	44	72	74	63	30				
		1-2 T	(musical notation)	72	78	91	80	19				
		2-2 T-B	(musical notation)	69	82	93	81	24				
		2-2 T	(musical notation)	37	52	74	54	37				
		2-2 B	(musical notation)	44	69	76	63	32				
		2-2 T-B	(musical notation)	37	50	70	52	33	69	26	M	T
		2-2 T	(musical notation)	57	74	87	73	30				
		3-2 T-B	(musical notation)	65	82	93	80	28				
		3-2 B	(musical notation)	48	67	87	67	39				
		3-2 T-B	(musical notation)	57	72	87	72	30				
		3-2 T	(musical notation)	13	19	26	19	13				
		3-2 B	(musical notation)	57	70	87	71	30				
		4-2 T-B	(musical notation)		80	82	81	2				
		1-3	(musical notation)	58	73	79	70	21				
		1-3	(musical notation)	72	80	93	82	21				
		1-3	(musical notation)	67	76	84	76	17				
		2-3	(musical notation)	66	76	83	75	17				

[161]

Number	Pattern	Level Test ITML	Item	Difficulty 4-6	7-9	10-12	Comp.	Growth	Over-all Diff.	Over-all Growth	Category Diff.	Category Growth
		2-3	(music notation)	57	68	75	67	18				
		2-3	(music notation)	57	68	77	67	20.				
		2-3	(music notation)	61	77	79	72	18				
		3-3	(music notation)	66	72	84	74	18	70	19	M	T
		3-3	(music notation)	69	80	93	81	24				
		3-3	(music notation)	69	80	82	77	13				
		3-3	(music notation)	68	76	82	75	14				
		4-3	(music notation)		70	91	81	21				
		4-3	(music notation)		34	71	53	37				
		4-3	(music notation)		30	40	35	10				
3	(music notation)	2-1	(music notation)	52	74	85	70	33				
		3-1	(music notation)	48	52	72	57	24	64	29	M	VH
		3-2 T-B	(music notation)	13	19	26	19	13	19	13	VD	L
		1-3	(music notation)	58	73	79	70	21				
		2-3	(music notation)	66	76	83	75	17	73	19	M	T
4	(music notation)	1-1	(music notation)	80	87	94	87	14				
		1-1	(music notation)	37	46	54	46	17				
		1-1	(music notation)	50	54	61	55	11				
		1-1	(music notation)	56	69	72	66	16				
		2-1	(music notation)	46	48	67	54	21				
		2-1	(music notation)	54	56	64	58	10	59	14	M	T
		2-1	(music notation)	63	72	89	75	26				
		3-1	(music notation)	50	52	58	53	8				

Number	Pattern	ITML	Item	4-6	7-9	10-12	Comp.	Growth	Diff.	Growth	Diff.	Growth
			Difficulty						**Over-all**		**Category**	
		3-1	♪	50	58	65	58	15				
		3-1	♪	54	58	63	58	9				
		4-1	♪		32	43	38	11				
		1-2 T	♪	83	91	94	89	11				
		1-2 T-B	♪	78	87	89	85	11				
		1-2 T-B	♪	72	87	89	83	17				
		1-2 T-B	♪	70	82	89	80	19				
		1-2 T-B	♪	83	89	94	89	11				
		2-2 T-B	♪	72	83	96	84	24				
		2-2 B	♪	37	52	74	54	37	81	18	M	T
		2-2 T-B	♪	72	83	93	83	21				
		2-2 T-B	♪	74	82	93	83	19				
		2-2 T-B	♪	57	74	87	73	30				
		3-2 T-B	♪	65	82	93	80	28				
		3-2 T-B	♪	69	80	89	79	20				
		4-2 T-B	♪		82	85	84	3				
		4-2 B	♪		82	83	83	1				
		1-3	♪	72	80	93	82	21	84	19	M	T
		1-3	♪	77	87	93	86	16				
6	♪	1-1	♪	80	87	94	87	14				
		1-1	♪	37	46	54	46	17	66	16	M	T
		1-1	♪	56	69	72	66	16				

[163]

Number	Pattern	Level Test ITML	Item	4-6	7-9	10-12	Comp.	Growth	Diff. (Over-all)	Growth (Over-all)	Diff. (Category)	Growth (Category)
		1-2 B		78	87	89	85	11				
		3-2 T-B		65	82	93	80	28	83	14	M	L
		4-2 T			82	85	84	3				
		1-3		77	87	93	86	16	86	16	E	T
7		4-1			46	52	49	6	49	6	D	VL
		3-2 T		57	72	87	72	30	77	16	M	T
		4-2 T-B			80	82	81	2				
		4-3			34	71	53	37	53	37	VD	VH
8		1-1		80	87	94	87	14				
		1-1		37	46	54	46	17	64	17	M	T
		1-1		59	69	72	66	16				
		1-1		39	43	61	58	22				
		1-2 T-B		78	87	89	85	11	82	20	M	T
		3-2 T-B		65	82	93	80	28				
		1-3		77	87	93	86	16				
		3-3		66	72	84	74	18	80	81	M	T
		4-3			70	91	80	21				
9		4-1			46	52	49	6	49	6	D	VL
		4-2 T-B			80	82	81	2	81	2	M	VL
10		2-2 T		44	69	76	63	32	63	32	D	H

Number	Pattern	Level Test ITML	Item	Difficulty 4-6	7-9	10-12	Comp.	Growth	Over-all Diff.	Over-all Growth	Category Diff.	Category Growth
11	(notation)	1-1	(notation)	68	82	93	81	25				
		2-1	(notation)	32	52	56	47	24	59	21	M	T
		2-1	(notation)	48	54	78	60	30				
		4-1	(notation)		46	52	49	6				
		1-2 T-B	(notation)	72	96	98	89	26				
		2-2 T-B	(notation)	69	82	93	81	24				
		2-2 B	(notation)	44	69	76	63	32	67	19	M	T
		3-2 T	(notation)	13	19	26	19	13				
		4-2 T-B	(notation)		80	82	81	2				
		2-3	(notation)	61	77	79	72	18				
		3-3	(notation)	69	80	82	77	13				
		4-3	(notation)		70	91	80	21				
		4-3	(notation)		30	40	35	10				
12	(notation)	1-1	(notation)	68	82	93	81	25	70	20	E	T
		3-1	(notation)	50	58	65	58	15				
		1-2 T-B	(notation)	72	96	98	87	26	87	26	E	T
		1-3	(notation)	72	80	93	82	21	83	17	M	T
		3-3	(notation)	79	80	92	84	13				
13	(notation)	1-1	(notation)	68	82	93	81	25				
		2-1	(notation)	32	52	56	47	24				
		2-1	(notation)	48	54	78	60	30				
		3-1	(notation)	48	50	57	52	9	55	18	M	T
		4-1	(notation)		32	43	38	11				
		4-1	(notation)		46	62	49	6				

Number	Pattern	Level Test ITML	Item	Difficulty 4-6	7-9	10-12	Comp.	Growth	Over-all Diff.	Over-all Growth	Category Diff.	Category Growth
		1-2 T-B		72	96	98	89	26				
		2-2 T-B		69	82	93	81	24				
		2-2 T		37	52	74	54	37	65	22	M	T
		2-2 B		44	69	76	63	32				
		3-2 T		13	18	26	19	13				
		4-2 T-B			80	82	81	2				
		2-3		61	77	79	72	18				
		3-3		69	80	82	77	13	66	16	M	T
		4-3			70	91	81	21				
		4-3			30	40	35	10				
14		1-1		68	82	93	81	25	70	20	E	T
		3-1		50	58	65	58	15				
		1-2 T-B		72	96	98	89	25	89	26	E	T
		1-3		72	80	93	82	21	80	17	M	T
		3-3		69	80	82	77	13				
15		1-2 T		83	91	94	89	11	81	22	M	T
		2-2 T-B		57	74	87	73	30				
		3-3		69	80	93	81	24	81	24	M	H
16		3-1		50	52	58	53	8				
		3-1		61	67	74	67	13	62	15	M	T
		3-1		54	65	78	66	24				
		1-2 T		83	91	94	89	11	81	22	M	T
		2-2 T		57	74	87	73	30				

Number	Level Test Pattern	Level Test ITML	Item	Difficulty 4-6	7-9	10-12	Comp.	Growth	Over-all Diff.	Growth	Category Diff.	Growth
		1-3		72	80	93	82	21				
		1-3		77	87	93	86	16	83	20	M	T
		3-3		69	80	93	81	24				
17		3-1		54	65	78	66	24	66	24	M	H
		1-2 T		83	91	98	91	15				
		2-2 T		57	74	87	73	30	78	25	M	T
		3-2 T-B		57	70	87	71	30				
23		1-1		48	56	61	55	13	52	18	D	T
		1-1		39	43	61	48	22				
		1-2 B		76	83	87	82	11	83	14	M	L
		2-2 B		76	83	93	84	17				
24		2-2 T		44	69	76	63	32	63	32	D	H
25		2-1		39	57	59	52	20	52	20	D	T
		2-2 T-B		70	72	89	77	19	77	19	M	T
26		1-1		68	82	93	81	25	71	28	E	VH
		2-1		48	54	78	60	30				
		1-2 T-B		72	96	98	89	26	76	29	M	H
		2-2 B		44	69	76	63	32				
		3-3		69	80	82	77	13	77	13	M	L
30		3-1		50	52	58	53	8				
		3-1		61	67	74	67	13	62	15	M	T
		3-1		54	65	78	66	24				

Number	Pattern	Level Test ITML	Item	4-6	7-9	10-12	Comp.	Growth	Over-all Diff.	Over-all Growth	Category Diff.	Category Growth
		1-2 T		83	91	94	89	11				
		2-2 T		57	74	87	73	30	79	25	M	T
		3-2 T-B		65	82	93	80	28				
		3-2 B		57	70	87	71	30				
		1-3		39	57	72	56	33				
		3-3		66	72	84	74	18	55	25	VD	H
		4-3			34	71	53	37				
		4-3			30	40	35	10				
31		1-1		68	82	93	81	25				
		2-1		32	52	56	47	24				
		2-1		48	54	78	60	30	58	19	M	T
		3-1		48	50	57	52	9				
		4-1			46	52	49	6				
		1-2 T-B		72	96	98	89	26				
		2-2 T-B		69	82	93	81	25				
		2-2 B		44	69	76	63	32	67	20	M	T
		3-2 T		13	19	26	19	13				
		4-2 T-B			80	82	81	2				
		2-3		61	77	79	72	18	54	14	VD	L
		4-3			30	40	35	10				
32		1-1		68	82	93	81	25	70	20	E	T
		3-1		50	58	65	58	15				
		1-2 T-B		72	96	98	87	26	87	26	E	T

Number	Pattern	Level Test / ITML	Item	Difficulty 4-6	7-9	10-12	Comp.	Growth	Over-all Diff.	Over-all Growth	Category Diff.	Category Growth
34	♪	1-1	♪	80	87	94	87	14				
		1-1	♪	37	46	54	46	17	66	16	M	T
		1-1	♪	56	69	72	66	16				
		1-2 T-B	♪	78	87	89	85	11				
		1-2 T-B	♪	83	89	94	87	11	84	17	M	T
		3-2 T-B	♪	65	82	93	80	28				
		1-3	♪	77	87	93	86	16	86	16	E	T
36	♪	1-1	♪	80	87	94	87	14				
		1-1	♪	37	46	54	46	17	66	16	M	T
		1-1	♪	56	69	72	66	16				
		1-2 T-B	♪	78	87	89	85	11				
		1-2 T-B	♪	83	89	94	87	11	84	17	M	T
		3-2 T-B	♪	65	82	93	80	29				
		1-3	♪	77	87	93	86	16	86	16	E	T
38	♪	1-1	♪	80	87	94	87	14				
		1-1	♪	37	46	54	46	17	66	16	M	T
		1-1	♪	56	69	72	66	16				
		1-2 T-B	♪	78	87	89	85	11				
		1-2 T-B	♪	83	89	94	87	11	84	17	M	T
		3-2 T-B	♪	65	82	93	80	28				
		1-3	♪	77	87	93	86	16	86	16	E	T
41	♪	4-1	♪	46	52	49	6		49	6	D	VL
		4-2 T-B	♪	80	82	81	2		81	2	M	VL

[169]

Complex Minor Tonal Patterns
Expanded Harmonic Functions

Number	Pattern	Level Test ITML	Item	4-6	7-9	10-12	Comp.	Growth	Diff.	Growth	Diff.	Growth
				Difficulty					Over-all		Category	
1		2-1		44	62	67	58	23	58	23	M	L
		2-2 T-B		67	74	98	80	31	82	26	M	T
		2-2 T		72	83	93	83	21				
2		2-1		32	52	56	47	24	47	24	D	T
		2-2 B		69	82	93	81	24	81	24	M	T
7		2-2 T-B		63	74	89	75	26	75	26	M	T
8		2-1		63	72	89	75	26	75	26	E	T
13		2-2 T-B		65	82	96	81	31	81	31	M	H
14		2-1		48	54	78	60	30	60	30	M	H
		2-2 T-B		44	69	76	63	32	63	32	VD	H
15		1-2 T-B		72	87	89	83	17	83	17	M	L

[170]

APPENDIX C

Basic Duple Rhythm Patterns
Tempo and Meter Beats

Number	Pattern	Level Test ITML	Item	\bf Difficulty 4-6	7-9	10-12	Comp.	Growth	Over-all Diff.	Growth	Category Diff.	Growth
1	[notation]	3-1	[notation]	60	69	72	67	12				
		3-1	[notation]	44	46	49	46	5	57	8	D	L
		1-3	[notation]	48	59	69	59	21				
		1-3	[notation]	62	69	72	68	10	64	10	E	L
2	[notation]	1-1	[notation]	83	96	98	92	15				
		2-1	[notation]	57	80	82	73	25				
		2-1	[notation]	41	44	69	51	28				
		2-1	[notation]	43	44	57	48	14				
		2-1	[notation]	44	52	59	52	15				
		2-1	[notation]	54	57	60	57	6	63	16	M	T
		2-1	[notation]	54	67	80	67	27				
		3-1	[notation]	46	48	56	50	10				
		3-1	[notation]	63	82	91	79	28				
		4-1	[notation]		61	63	62	2				
		1-2 T	[notation]	59	78	80	72	21				
		1-2 B	[notation]	69	74	80	74	11	73	16	E	T
		1-3	[notation]	62	68	82	71	20				
		1-3	[notation]	62	69	72	68	10				
		1-3	[notation]	40	47	53	47	13	54	12	D	H
		2-3	[notation]	27	32	33	31	6				

Number	Pattern	Level Test ITML	Item	\[4-6\]	\[7-9\]	\[10-12\]	Comp.	Growth	Over-all Diff.	Over-all Growth	Category Diff.	Category Growth
3	[notation]	1-1	[notation]	83	96	98	92	15				
		1-1	[notation]	67	69	70	69	3				
		1-1	[notation]	43	67	69	60	26				
		1-1	[notation]	61	70	76	69	15				
		1-1	[notation]	52	54	72	59	20				
		1-1	[notation]	33	50	59	47	26				
		2-1	[notation]	48	59	80	62	32	64	16	M	T
		2-1	[notation]	541	56	57	56	3				
		2-1	[notation]	32	44	59	45	27				
		3-1	[notation]	60	69	72	67	12				
		3-1	[notation]	64	70	74	69	10				
		4-1	[notation]		69	72	70	3				
		1-2 T	[notation]	59	78	80	72	21				
		1-2 T-B	[notation]	59	72	74	68	15				
		1-2 T-B	[notation]	54	61	76	64	22				
		1-2 B	[notation]	69	74	80	74	11				
		1-2 T-B	[notation]	74	78	85	79	11				
		1-2 T	[notation]	72	78	89	80	17	68	18	M	T
		1-2 T	[notation]	28	63	65	52	37				
		1-2 T-B	[notation]	76	80	82	79	6				
		2-2 T-B	[notation]	56	58	70	61	14				

[174]

Number	Level Test Pattern	Level Test ITML	Item	Difficulty 4-6	7-9	10-12	Comp.	Growth	Over-all Diff.	Growth	Category Diff.	Growth
		2-2 B		48	70	78	65	30				
		2-2 T-B		54	56	63	58	19				
4		1-2 T		54	61	76	64	22	62	18	D	T
		2-2 T		56	58	70	61	14				

Basic Duple Rhythm Patterns
Fractionations and Elongations

Number	Level Pattern	Level Test ITML	Level Item	Difficulty 4-6	7-9	10-12	Comp.	Growth	Over-all Diff.	Over-all Growth	Category Diff.	Category Growth
1	[notation]	1-1	[notation]	43	67	69	60	26				
		3-1	[notation]	44	46	49	46	5				
		3-1	[notation]	59	67	76	67	17	60	12	M	T
		4-1	[notation]		65	69	67	4				
		4-1	[notation]		54	61	58	7				
		1-2 B	[notation]	59	78	80	72	21				
		1-2 T	[notation]	59	72	74	68	15				
		1-2 T	[notation]	69	74	80	74	11				
		1-2 T	[notation]	44	62	63	56	19				
		2-2 T-B	[notation]	70	72	91	78	21				
		2-2 B	[notation]	39	52	65	52	26	67	19	M	L
		2-2 T	[notation]	48	70	78	65	30				
		2-2 T-B	[notation]	70	72	96	79	26				
		3-2 B	[notation]	46	54	63	54	17				
		4-2 T	[notation]		63	70	67	7				
		4-2 B	[notation]		61	72	67	11				
		4-3	[notation]		58	62	60	4	60	4	E	VL

[176]

Number	Pattern	Level Test ITML	Item	4-6	7-9	10-12	Comp.	Growth	Diff.	Growth	Diff.	Growth
									Over-all		Category	
2	[music]	4-1	[music]		69	72	70	3	70	3	E	L
		1-2 T	[music]	52	70	80	67	28	67	28	M	H
		2-3	[music]	52	58	64	58	12	58	12	M	T
3	[music]	1-1	[music]	32	48	50	43	18				
		1-1	[music]	43	56	61	53	18				
		1-1	[music]	48	63	69	60	21	57	15	M	T
		4-1	[music]		69	72	70	3				
		4-1	[music]		52	65	59	13				
		1-2 T-B	[music]	74	78	85	79	11				
		1-2 T	[music]	44	62	63	56	19				
		1-2 B	[music]	52	70	80	64	28	58	19	M	L
		3-2 T	[music]	44	69	74	62	30				
		4-2 T-B	[music]		24	33	29	9				
4	[music]	1-1	[music]	43	65	68	59	25				
		3-1	[music]	64	70	74	69	10	62	16	M	T
		4-1	[music]		52	65	59	13				
		1-2 B	[music]	59	72	74	68	15	72	27	E	H
		3-2 B	[music]	57	76	96	76	39				
		2-3	[music]	52	58	64	58	12	58	12	M	T

[177]

Number	Pattern	Level Test ITML	Item	Difficulty 4-6	7-9	10-12	Comp.	Growth	Over-all Diff.	Growth	Category Diff.	Growth
5	(notation)	1-1	(notation)	43	65	68	59	25	59	25	M	H
		1-2 B	(notation)	59	72	74	68	15	66	22	M	T
		2-2 T	(notation)	48	70	78	65	30				
6	(notation)	1-1	(notation)	67	69	70	69	3	68	4	E	L
		4-1	(notation)		65	69	67	4				
		1-2 T-B	(notation)	33	50	59	47	26	44	24	VD	T
		2-2 T	(notation)	39	52	65	52	26				
		3-2 B	(notation)	24	35	44	34	20				
		2-3	(notation)	52	58	64	58	12	58	12	M	T

Basic Duple Rhythm Patterns
Upbeats

Number	Level Pattern	Level Test ITML	Item	Difficulty 4-6	7-9	10-12	Comp.	Growth	Over-all Diff.	Growth	Category Diff.	Growth
1	(notation)	1-1	(notation)	65	67	87	73	22	76	25	E	H
		3-1	(notation)	63	82	91	79	28				
		1-2 T-B	(notation)	59	69	80	69	21	69	21	E	T
		2-3	(notation)	27	32	37	32	10	32	10	D	H
3	(notation)	1-1	(notation)	48	63	69	60	21	64	19	M	T
		3-1	(notation)	59	67	76	67	17				
		1-2 T	(notation)	44	62	63	56	19				
		1-2 T-B	(notation)	52	70	80	67	28	60	24	D	H
		2-2 B	(notation)	44	67	74	62	30				
		3-2 B	(notation)	46	54	63	54	17				
4	(notation)	1-1	(notation)	32	48	50	43	18	43	18	D	T
		1-2 T-B	(notation)	50	70	72	64	22	64	22	M	T
		2-3	(notation)	27	32	33	31	6	46	5	E	L
		4-3	(notation)		58	62	60	4				
5	(notation)	4-1	(notation)		54	61	58	7	58	7	M	L

Complex Duple Rhythm Patterns
Fractionations and Elongations

Number	Pattern	Level Test ITML	Item	Difficulty 4-6	7-9	10-12	Comp.	Growth	Over-all Diff.	Growth	Category Diff.	Growth
1	♩	2-1	♩ ♫♫	57	80	82	73	25	73	25	E	T
		2-2 T	♩ ♫♫♫	39	52	65	52	26				
		2-2 T-B	♩ ♬♬	72	73	96	80	24	65	26	M	T
		2-2 T	♩ ♪♫ ♪	52	67	76	65	24				
		2-2 B	♪♩ ♫♫	44	67	74	62	30				
2	♩· ♪	1-1	♪♩· ♪♫♪	65	67	87	73	22	70	24	E	T
		2-1	♩· ♪♫♫	54	67	80	67	26				
		1-2 T-B	♪♩· ♪♫♫	59	69	80	69	21	69	21	M	T
		1-3	♩· ♪♩·	57	70	72	66	15	66	15	E	T
3	♪♩·	1-1	♪♩· ♫♫	52	54	72	59	20	59	20	M	T
		1-2 B	♪♩· ♫♫	28	63	65	52	37	52	37	D	H
4	♪♩ ♪	1-1	♪♩ ♪♫♫	61	70	76	69	15	60	12	M	L
		3-1	♪♩ ♪♫♫	46	48	56	50	10				
		1-2 B	♪♩ ♪♫♫	54	61	76	64	22	68	29	M	T
		3-2 B	♪♩ ♪♬	54	74	89	72	35				
		1-3	♪♩ ♪♩ ♩	48	59	69	59	21	59	21	M	H
5	♫♫ ♫♫	4-2 B	♫♫ ♫♫♫♬♪		61	72	66	11	66	11	M	L

Number	Pattern	Level Test ITML	Item	Difficulty 4-6	7-9	10-12	Comp.	Growth	Over-all Diff.	Growth	Category Diff.	Growth
6	[music notation]	2-1	[music notation]	41	44	69	51	28	51	28	M	T
		2-2 T-B	[music notation]	56	58	70	61	14	61	14	M	L
		2-3	[music notation]	46	48	55	50	9	50	9	D	T
7	[music notation]	2-2 B	[music notation]	58	70	78	65	30	65	30	M	T
8	[music notation]	1-2 B	[music notation]	72	78	89	80	17	80	17	E	L
		2-3	[music notation]	46	48	55	50	9	50	9	D	T
9	[music notation]	2-1	[music notation]	44	52	59	52	15	52	15	M	L
10	[music notation]	2-1	[music notation]	48	59	80	62	32	62	32	M	H
12	[music notation]	2-2 T	[music notation]	59	65	87	70	29	70	28	M	T
13	[music notation]	2-1	[music notation]	32	44	59	45	27	45	27	D	T

Complex Duple Rhythm Patterns
Rests

Number	Pattern	Level Test ITML	Item	4-6	7-9	10-12	Comp.	Growth	Diff.	Growth	Diff.	Growth
				Difficulty					Over-all		Category	
1	[notation]	1-2 B	[notation]	59	78	80	72	21				
		1-2 T	[notation]	59	72	74	68	15				
		1-2 T	[notation]	69	74	80	74	11	66	23	M	H
		1-2 T	[notation]	52	70	80	67	28				
		2-2 T	[notation]	26	47	67	47	41				
		1-3	[notation]	54	66	72	64	18	64	18	E	H
2	[notation]	1-2 T	[notation]	72	78	89	80	17				
		1-2 T-B	[notation]	50	70	72	64	22				
		3-2 B	[notation]	57	76	96	76	39	71	19	E	T
		4-2 B	[notation]		67	72	70	5				
		4-2 B	[notation]		61	72	66	11				
		1-3	[notation]	62	68	82	71	20				
		1-3	[notation]	54	66	72	64	18				
		1-3	[notation]	56	64	72	64	16	56	14	D	L
		1-3	[notation]	40	47	53	47	13				
		2-3	[notation]	27	32	37	32	10				
		4-3	[notation]		58	62	60	4				

Number	Level Pattern	Level Test ITML	Item	Difficulty 4-6	7-9	10-12	Comp.	Growth	Over-all Diff.	Over-all Growth	Category Diff.	Category Growth
3	♩ (2/4 pattern)	1-2 B	(musical notation)	74	78	85	79	11				
		1-2 T	(musical notation)	52	70	80	67	28	67	19	M	T
		3-2 B	(musical notation)	46	54	63	54	17				
4	♩ (2/4 pattern)	2-2 T-B	(musical notation)	54	56	63	58	9	58	9	M	L
6	♩ (2/4 pattern)	2-2 T-B	(musical notation)	70	72	91	78	21	72	26	E	H
		2-2 T	(musical notation)	48	70	78	65	30				
7	♩ (2/4 pattern)	2-2 T-B	(musical notation)	69	70	89	76	20	53	14	D	T
		4-2 T-B	(musical notation)		24	33	29	9				

Complex Duple Rhythm Patterns
Ties

Number	Level Pattern	Level ITML	Item	4-6	7-9	10-12	Comp.	Growth	Diff.	Growth	Diff.	Growth
				Difficulty					Over-all		Category	
1	[notation]	2-3	[notation]	56	58	63	59	7	59	7	E	H
2	[notation]	2-1	[notation]	52	59	70	60	18	64	20	M	T
		2-1	[notation]	57	72	78	69	21				
		2-2 B	[notation]	70	73	89	77	19	70	18	E	L
		2-2 T-B	[notation]	46	57	74	59	28				
		4-2 T-B	[notation]		70	76	73	6				
		2-3	[notation]	23	26	30	26	7	43	6	D	L
		4-3	[notation]		58	62	60	4				
9	[notation]	2-2 B	[notation]	52	67	76	65	24	65	24	M	T
10	[notation]	2-1	[notation]	54	56	57	56	3	56	3	D	L
		3-2 T	[notation]	44	69	74	62	30	62	30	M	II
11	[notation]	2-1	[notation]	57	72	78	69	21	69	21	E	T
		2-2 T-B	[notation]	46	57	74	59	28	59	28	D	T

Complex Duple Rhythm Patterns
Upbeats

Number	Pattern	Level Test ITML	Item	Difficulty 4-6	7-9	10-12	Comp.	Growth	Over-all Diff.	Growth	Category Diff.	Growth
1		4-1			61	63	62	2	62	2	M	L
		2-2 T-B		69	70	89	76	20	74	13	E	L
		4-2 T-B			70	76	73	6				
3		2-1		43	44	57	48	14	48	14	D	T
5		2-1		57	72	78	69	21	69	21	E	H
		2-2 B		46	57	74	59	28	60	25	D	H
		3-2 T-B		50	57	72	60	22				

[185]

Basic Triple Rhythm Patterns
Tempo and Meter Beats

Number	Level Pattern	Level Test ITML	Item	4-6	7-9	10-12	Comp.	Growth	Over-all Diff.	Over-all Growth	Category Diff.	Category Growth
1	[notation]	3-1	[notation]	61	63	65	63	4	63	4	M	L
		1-2 T	[notation]	28	63	65	52	37	62	30	M	H
		2-2 T	[notation]	57	76	80	71	23				
		1-3	[notation]	71	80	91	81	20	81	20	E	T
2	[notation]	1-1	[notation]	76	83	85	81	9				
		2-1	[notation]	44	52	54	50	10				
		2-1	[notation]	50	57	69	59	19	61	12	M	T
		3-1	[notation]	52	55	59	55	7				
		4-1	[notation]		54	67	61	13				
		1-2 T-B	[notation]	61	83	91	78	30				
		3-2 T-B	[notation]	59	74	91	75	32	71	27	M	T
		3-2 T	[notation]	52	59	70	60	18				
		1-3	[notation]	71	80	91	81	20	74	20	M	T
		1-3	[notation]	57	67	77	67	20				
3	[notation]	1-1	[notation]	76	83	85	81	9				
		1-1	[notation]	72	76	82	77	10				
		1-1	[notation]	64	69	70	68	6				

[186]

Number	Pattern	Level Test ITML	Item	4-6	7-9	10-12	Comp.	Growth	Over-all Diff.	Over-all Growth	Category Diff.	Category Growth
		1-1	*(musical notation)*	50	57	59	55	9				
		1-1	*(musical notation)*	61	67	70	66	9				
		1-1	*(musical notation)*	65	67	70	67	5				
		1-1	*(musical notation)*	67	69	78	71	11				
		1-1	*(musical notation)*	65	70	83	73	18				
		2-1	*(musical notation)*	65	72	76	71	11				
		2-1	*(musical notation)*	65	72	75	71	10	63	11	M	T
		2-1	*(musical notation)*	32	39	56	42	24				
		2-1	*(musical notation)*	54	59	60	58	6				
		2-1	*(musical notation)*	46	57	59	54	13				
		2-1	*(musical notation)*	52	54	69	58	17				
		2-1	*(musical notation)*	37	41	46	41	9				
		3-1	*(musical notation)*	48	50	69	56	21				
		3-1	*(musical notation)*	61	63	65	63	4				
		4-1	*(musical notation)*		54	61	58	7				
		4-1	*(musical notation)*		76	82	79	6				
		4-1	*(musical notation)*		50	67	59	17				
		1-2 T-B	*(musical notation)*	72	82	91	82	19				
		1-2 B	*(musical notation)*	72	76	82	77	10				

Number	Pattern	Level Test ITML	Item	Difficulty 4-6	7-9	10-12	Comp.	Growth	Over-all Diff.	Growth	Category Diff.	Growth
		1-2 B	♪ [musical notation]	48	50	67	55	19				
		1-2 B	♪ [musical notation]	32	48	50	43	18				
		1-2 B	♪ [musical notation]	52	54	72	59	20	62	19	M	T
		2-2 T	♪ [musical notation]	70	73	89	77	19				
		2-2 T-B	♪ [musical notation]	46	63	78	62	32				
		3-2 T	♪ [musical notation]	54	69	71	65	17				
		3-2 T	♪ [musical notation]	31	37	46	38	15				
		3-2 T	♪ [musical notation]	52	59	70	60	18				
		1=3	♪ [musical notation]	51	66	73	63	22	63	18	D	L
		2-3	♪ [musical notation]	57	62	71	63	14				
4	♪ [musical notation]	3-1	♪ [musical notation]	48	50	69	56	21	56	21	D	H
		2-2 T	♪ [musical notation]	74	82	91	82	17	82	17	E	L

Basic Triple Rhythm Patterns
Fractionations and Elongations

Number	Level Pattern	Test ITML	Item	Difficulty 4-6	7-9	10-12	Comp.	Growth	Over-all Diff.	Growth	Category Diff.	Growth
1	[notation]	1-1	[notation]	64	69	70	68	6	68	6	M	L
		1-2 B	[notation]	61	76	85	74	24				
		1-2 T	[notation]	26	69	74	56	48	66	30	M	T
		4-2 T	[notation]		59	78	69	19				
		2-3	[notation]	33	34	40	36	7	49	5	M	T
		4-3	[notation]		61	64	62	3				
2	[notation]	1-1	[notation]	65	70	83	73	18	73	18	E	T
		1-2 B	[notation]	44	62	63	56	19	56	17	D	T
		4-2 T	[notation]		48	63	56	15				
		2-3	[notation]	60	62	63	62	3	46	4	M	T
		2-3	[notation]	28	31	32	30	4				
3	[notation]	1-2 T	[notation]	70	73	89	77	19	68	24	M	T
		1-2 B	[notation]	46	57	74	59	28				
4	[notation]	1-1	[notation]	65	70	83	73	18	73	18	E	T
		1-2 B	[notation]	44	62	63	56	19	56	19	D	T
		2-3	[notation]	28	31	32	30	4	30	4	D	T

[189]

Number	Pattern	Level Test ITML	Item	Difficulty 4-6	7-9	10-12	Comp.	Growth	Over-all Diff.	Growth	Category Diff.	Growth
5	[notation]	1-1	[notation]	61	67	70	66	9	66	9	M	T
		1-2 T	[notation]	46	74	78	66	32				
		1-2 T-B	[notation]	56	66	68	63	12	62	18	M	T
		2-2 T	[notation]	54	56	63	58	9				
6	[notation]	1-1	[notation]	61	67	70	66	9	66	9	M	T
		1-2 B	[notation]	26	69	74	56	48	56	48	D	VH
7	[notation]	4-2 T	[notation]		59	78	69	19	69	19	M	T
8	[notation]	1-1	[notation]	54	59	72	62	18				
		1-1	[notation]	48	50	67	55	19				
		1-1	[notation]	50	57	59	55	9				
		1-1	[notation]	32	59	60	50	18				
		2-1	[notation]	48	50	52	50	4				
		2-1	[notation]	54	59	60	58	6	61	13	M	T
		2-1	[notation]	52	54	69	58	17				
		3-1	[notation]	69	70	76	72	7				
		3-1	[notation]	52	55	59	55	7				
		4-1	[notation]		63	82	73	19				
		4-1	[notation]		76	82	79	6				

Number	Level			Difficulty					Over-all		Category	
	Pattern	Test ITML	Item	4-6	7-9	10-12	Comp.	Growth	Diff.	Growth	Diff.	Growth
		1-2 T	*[musical notation]*	61	76	85	74	24				
		1-2 T-B	*[musical notation]*	69	76	80	75	11				
		1-2 T-B	*[musical notation]*	63	82	85	77	22				
		1-2 T-B	*[musical notation]*	26	69	74	56	48				
		1-2 T	*[musical notation]*	48	63	70	60	52				
		1-2 T	*[musical notation]*	28	63	65	52	37				
		1-2 T-B	*[musical notation]*	52	74	76	67	24				
		1-2 T-B	*[musical notation]*	56	66	68	63	12				
		2-2 B	*[musical notation]*	74	82	91	82	17	64	24	M	T
		2-2 T-B	*[musical notation]*	63	69	70	67	7				
		2-2 T-B	*[musical notation]*	62	67	69	66	7				
		2-2 B	*[musical notation]*	41	48	61	50	20				
		2-2 T-B	*[musical notation]*	46	63	78	62	32				
		2-2 T-B	*[musical notation]*	52	54	83	63	31				
		3-2 T	*[musical notation]*	44	69	71	61	27				
		3-2 T	*[musical notation]*	31	37	46	38	15				
		3-2 B	*[musical notation]*	44	72	78	65	34				
		4-2 T-B	*[musical notation]*		65	69	67	4				

[191]

Number	Pattern	Level Test ITML	Item	Difficulty 4-6	7-9	10-12	Comp.	Growth	Over-all Diff.	Over-all Growth	Category Diff.	Category Growth
		1-3	(musical notation)	51	66	73	63	22				
		1-3	(musical notation)	57	70	73	67	16				
		1-3	(musical notation)	57	67	77	67	20	60	12	E	H
		2-3	(musical notation)	60	62	63	62	3				
		2-3	(musical notation)	33	34	37	35	4				
		3-3	(musical notation)	62	63	69	65	7				
9	(musical notation)	1-1	(musical notation)	32	59	60	50	28	50	28	VD	VH
		1-2 T	(musical notation)	26	69	74	56	48	64	36	M	H
		2-2 T-B	(musical notation)	57	76	80	71	23				
		1-3	(musical notation)	57	70	73	67	16	48	10	M	H
		2-3	(musical notation)	28	31	32	30	4				
10	(musical notation)	1-1	(musical notation)	65	67	70	67	5	67	5	M	L
		1-2 B	(musical notation)	46	74	78	66	32	67	20	M	T
		4-2 B	(musical notation)		63	72	68	9				
12	(musical notation)	1-1	(musical notation)	72	76	82	77	10				
		2-1	(musical notation)	46	57	59	54	13				
		2-1	(musical notation)	52	54	69	58	17	59	12	M	T
		3-1	(musical notation)	25	34	44	34	19				
		4-1	(musical notation)		70	72	71	2				

Number	Pattern	Level Test ITML	Item	Difficulty 4-6	7-9	10-12	Comp.	Growth	Over-all Diff.	Growth	Category Diff.	Growth
		1-2 T	♪ (notation)	72	82	91	82	19				
		1-2 T	♪ (notation)	46	74	78	66	32	77	24	VE	T
		2-2 B	♪ (notation)	74	80	94	83	20				
		2-3	♪ (notation)	60	62	63	62	3	62	3	E	L
13	♪ (notation)	2-2 T	♪ (notation)	52	72	80	68	28	68	28	M	T
17	♪ (notation)	1-1	♪ (notation)	50	57	59	55	9	60	12	M	T
		4-1	♪ (notation)		56	72	64	16				
		1-2 T-B	♪ (notation)	56	66	68	63	12				
		3-2 T	♪ (notation)	44	69	71	61	27	64	16	M	L
		4-2 B	♪ (notation)		63	72	68	9				

Basic Triple Rhythm Patterns
Upbeats

Number	Pattern	Level Test ITML	Item	4-6	7-9	10-12	Comp.	Growth	Diff.	Growth	Diff.	Growth
1	[notation]	1-1	[notation]	54	59	72	62	18				
		3-1	[notation]	24	35	44	34	20				
		3-1	[notation]	52	55	59	55	7	59	13	M	T
		4-1	[notation]		63	82	73	19				
		4-1	[notation]		70	72	71	2				
		1-2 T	[notation]	69	76	80	75	11				
		1-2 T-B	[notation]	63	82	84	76	21	70	18	E	L
		3-2 T-B	[notation]	61	69	85	72	24				
		4-2 T	[notation]		48	63	56	15				
		2-3	[notation]	60	62	63	62	3	46	3	D	L
		2-3	[notation]	27	29	30	29	3				
2	[notation]	1-1	[notation]	48	50	67	55	19	55	19	D	H
		1-2 T	[notation]	48	63	70	60	22	64	23	D	H
		1-2 T-B	[notation]	52	74	76	67	24				
		3-3	[notation]	62	63	69	65	7	65	7	E	H
7	[notation]	4-1	[notation]		54	67	61	13	61	13	E	T

Complex Triple Rhythm Patterns
Fractionations and Elongations

Number	Pattern	Level Test ITML	Item	Difficulty 4-6	7-9	10-12	Comp.	Growth	Over-all Diff.	Growth	Category Diff.	Growth
1	*[notation]*	2-1	*[notation]*	44	52	54	50	10	50	10	D	T
		2-2 T	*[notation]*	52	72	80	68	28				
		2-2 T	*[notation]*	74	80	94	83	20	71	26	E	H
		2-2 B	*[notation]*	44	67	74	62	30				
6	*[notation]*	2-2 B	*[notation]*	41	48	61	50	20	50	20	D	T
8	*[notation]*	2-2 T-B	*[notation]*	63	69	70	67	7	67	7	M	L
9	*[notation]*	2-1	*[notation]*	54	59	60	58	6	58	6	M	L
		2-2 T-B	*[notation]*	46	63	78	62	32	64	18	M	T
		4-2 T-B	*[notation]*		65	69	67	4				
11	*[notation]*	2-1	*[notation]*	65	72	76	71	11	71	11	E	T

[195]

Complex Triple Rhythm Patterns
Rests

Number	Pattern	Test ITML	Item	4-6	7-9	10-12	Comp.	Growth	Diff. (Over-all)	Growth (Over-all)	Diff. (Category)	Growth (Category)
2	[notation]	1-2 T	[notation]	48	63	70	60	22	68	27	M	H
		3-2 T-B	[notation]	59	74	91	75	32				
		1-3	[notation]	54	66	72	64	18	66	17	E	H
		1-3	[notation]	57	70	73	67	16				
3	[notation]	1-2 T-B	[notation]	52	74	76	67	24	67	24	M	T
		1-3	[notation]	54	66	72	64	18				
		1-3	[notation]	60	67	73	66	13				
		1-3	[notation]	58	62	68	63	10	58	9	D	L
		2-3	[notation]	27	29	30	29	3				
		3-3	[notation]	62	63	69	65	7				
		4-3	[notation]		61	64	62	3				
5	[notation]	1-2 T-B	[notation]	61	83	91	78	30				
		1-2 T	[notation]	46	74	78	66	32	70	25	E	T
		2-2 T	[notation]	74	80	94	83	20				
		3-2 B	[notation]	46	52	63	54	17				
6	[notation]	2-2 T	[notation]	57	76	80	71	23	69	15	M	T
		2-2 T	[notation]	62	67	69	66	7				
7	[notation]	2-2 B	[notation]	62	67	69	66	7	66	7	D	L

Complex Triple Rhythm Patterns
Ties

Number	Level Pattern	Level Test ITML	Item	Difficulty 4-6	7-9	10-12	Comp.	Growth	Over-all Diff.	Over-all Growth	Category Diff.	Category Growth
2	(pattern)	2-1	(item)	37	57	60	51	23	51	23	M	T
		2-2 B	(item)	26	47	67	47	41				
		2-2 B	(item)	59	65	87	70	18	63	20	M	L
		4-2 B	(item)	71	72	72		1				
3	(pattern)	2-2 T	(item)	41	48	61	50	20	50	20	D	L
5	(pattern)	2-2 T	(item)	26	47	67	47	41				
		2-2 B	(item)	52	72	80	68	28	66	30	M	T
		2-2 B	(item)	74	80	94	83	20				
8	(pattern)	2-2 B	(item)	57	76	80	71	23	71	23	M	T
10	(pattern)	2-1	(item)	65	72	75	71	10				
		2-1	(item)	37	57	60	51	23	51	15	M	L
		4-1	(item)		54	67	61	13				
		2-2 B	(item)	74	82	91	82	17	76	23	E	T
		2-2 B	(item)	59	65	87	70	28				
11	(pattern)	3-2 B	(item)	44	72	78	65	34	65	34	M	H
13	(pattern)	2-1	(item)	32	39	56	42	24				
		2-1	(item)	37	41	46	41	9	49	22	D	T
		3-1	(item)	44	72	78	65	34				
		2-3	(item)	57	62	71	63	14	63	14	M	T

Complex Triple Rhythm Patterns
Upbeats

Number	Level Test			Difficulty					Over-all		Category	
	Pattern	ITML	Item	4-6	7-9	10-12	Comp.	Growth	Diff.	Growth	Diff.	Growth
1	𝄞	2-1	𝄞	48	50	52	50	4	54	10	M	L
		4-1	𝄞		50	67	58	17				
		2-2 T	𝄞	74	82	91	82	17	88	24	E	H
		2-2 T	𝄞	52	54	83	63	31				
2	𝄞	2-1	𝄞	50	57	69	59	19	59	19	D	T
5	𝄞	2-1	𝄞	37	57	60	51	23	51	23	D	H
		2-2 B	𝄞	59	65	87	70	28	62	22	D	¾
		3-2 B	𝄞	46	52	63	54	17				

[198]

APPENDIX D

Difficulty Level Taxonomy of Basic Major Tonal Patterns-Tonic Function

Aural Perception

Reading Recognition

Notational Understanding

Growth Rate Taxonomy of Basic Major Tonal Patterns-Tonic Function

Aural Perception

Reading Recognition

Notational Understanding

Difficulty Level Taxonomy of Baisc Major Tonal Patterns-Dominant Function

Aural Perception

Reading Recognition

Notational Understanding

Growth Rate Taxonomy of Basic Major Tonal Patterns-Dominant Function

Aural Perception

Reading Recognition

Notational Understanding

Difficulty Level Taxonomy of Basic Major Tonal Patterns-Subdominant Function

Aural Perception

Reading Recognition

Notational Understanding

Growth Rate Taxonomy of Basic Major Tonal Patterns-Subdominant Function
Aural Perception

Reading Recognition

Notational Understanding

Difficulty Level Taxonomy of Complex Major Tonal Patterns-Chromaticism

Aural Perception

Reading Recognition

Notational Understanding

Growth Rate Taxonomy of Complex Major Tonal Patterns-Chromaticism

Aural Perception

Reading Recognition

Notational Understanding

Difficulty Level Taxonomy of Complex Major Tonal Patterns-
Combined Harmonic Functions

Aural Perception

Reading Recognition

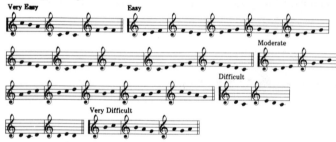

Notational Understanding

Growth Rate Taxonomy of Complex
Major Tonal Patterns-Combined Harmonic Functions

Aural Perception

Reading Recognition

Notational Understanding

Difficulty Level Taxonomy of Complex
Major Tonal Patterns-Expanded Harmonic Functions

Aural Perception

Reading Recognition

Notational Understanding

Growth Rate Taxonomy of Complex
Major Tonal Patterns-Expanded Harmonic Functions

Aural Perception

Reading Recognition

Notational Understanding

Difficulty Level Taxonomy of Basic Minor Tonal Patterns-Tonic Function

Aural Perception

Reading Recognition

Notational Understanding

Growth Rate Taxonomy of Basic Minor Tonal Patterns-Tonic Function

Aural Perception

Reading Recognition

Notational Understanding

Difficulty Level Taxonomy of Basic Minor Tonal Patterns-Dominant Function

Aural Perception

Reading Recognition

Notational Understanding

Growth Rate Taxonomy of Basic Minor Tonal Patterns-Dominant Function

Aural Perception

Reading Recognition

Notational Understanding

Difficulty Level Taxonomy of Basic Minor Tonal Patterns-Subdominant Function

Aural Perception

Reading Recognition

Notational Understanding

Growth Rate Taxonomy of Basic Minor Tonal Patterns-Subdominant Function

Aural Perception

Reading Recognition

Notational Understanding

Difficulty Level Taxonomy of Complex Minor Tonal Patterns-Chromaticism

Aural Perception

Reading Recognition

Notational Understanding

Growth Rate Taxonomy of Complex Minor Tonal Patterns-Chromaticism

Aural Perception

Reading Recognition

Notational Understanding

Difficulty Level Taxonomy of Complex
Minor Tonal Patterns-Combined Harmonic Functions

Aural Perception

Reading Recognition

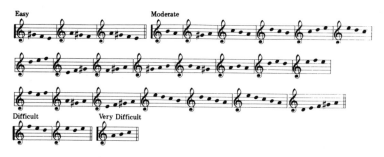

Notational Understanding

Growth Rate Taxonomy of Complex
Minor Tonal Patterns-Combined Harmonic Functions

Aural Perception

Reading Recognition

Notational Understanding

Difficulty Level Taxonomy of Complex

Minor Tonal Patterns-Expanded Harmonic Functions

Aural Perception

Reading Recognition

Growth Rate Taxonomy of Complex

Minor Tonal Patterns-Expanded Harmonic Functions

Aural Perception

Reading Recognition

APPENDIX E

Difficulty Level Taxonomy of Basic Duple
Rhythm Patterns-Tempo and Meter Beats

Aural Perception

Reading Recognition

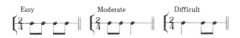

Notational Understanding

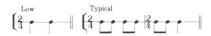

Growth Rate Taxonomy of Basic Duple
Rhythm Patterns-Tempo and Meter Beats

Aural Perception

Reading Recognition

Notational Understanding

Difficulty Taxonomy Level of Basic Duple
Rhythm Patterns-Fractionations and Elongations

Aural Perception

Reading Recognition

Notational Understanding

Growth Rate Taxonomy of Basic Duple
Rhythm Patterns-Fractionations and Elongations

Aural Perception

Reading Recognition

Notational Understanding

Difficulty Level Taxonomy of Basic Duple Rhythm Patterns-Upbeats

Aural Perception

Reading Recognition

Notational Understanding

Growth Rate Taxonomy of Basic Duple Rhythm Patterns-Upbeats

Aural Perception

Reading Recognition

Notational Understanding

Difficulty Level Taxonomy of Complex
Duple Rhythm Patterns-Fractionations and Elongations

Aural Perception

Reading Recognition

Notational Understanding

Growth Rate Taxonomy of Complex
Duple Rhythm Patterns-Fractionations and Elongations

Aural Perception

Reading Recognition

Notational Understanding

Difficulty Level Taxonomy of Complex Duple Rhythm Patterns-Rests

Reading Recognition

Notational Understanding

Growth Rate Taxonomy of Complex Duple Rhythm Patterns-Rests

Reading Recognition

Notational Understanding

Difficulty Level Taxonomy of Complex Duple Rhythm Patterns-Ties

Aural Perception

Reading Recognition

Notational Understanding

Growth Rate Taxonomy of Complex Duple Rhtyhm Patterns-Ties

Aural Perception

Reading Recognition

Notational Understanding

Difficulty Level Taxonomy of Complex Duple Rhythm Patterns-Upbeats

Aural Perception

Reading Recognition

Growth Rate Taxonomy of Complex Duple Rhythm Patterns-Upbeats

Aural Perception

Reading Recognition

Difficulty Level Taxonomy of Basic
Triple Rhythm Patterns-Tempo and Meter Beats

Aural Perception

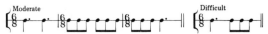

Reading Recognition

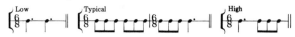

Notational Understanding

Growth Rate Taxonomy of Basic
Triple Rhythm Patterns-Tempo and Meter Beats

Aural Perception

Reading Recognition

Notational Understanding

Difficulty Level Taxonomy of Basic
Triple Rhythm Patterns-Fractionations and Elongations

Aural Perception

Reading Recognition

Notational Understanding

Growth Rate Taxonomy of Basic
Triple Rhythm Patterns-Fractionations and Elongations

Aural Perception

Reading Recognition

Notational Understanding

Difficulty Level Taxonomy of Basic Triple Rhythm Patterns-Upbeats

Aural Perception

Reading Recognition

Notational Understanding

Growth Rate Taxonomy of Basic Triple Rhythm Patterns

Aural Perception

Reading Recognition

Notational Understanding

Difficulty Level Taxonomy of Complex
Triple Rhythm Patterns-Fractionations and Elongations

Aural Perception

Reading Recognition

Growth Rate Taxonomy of Complex
Triple Rhythm Patterns—Fractionations and Elongations

Aural Perception

Reading Recognition

[229]

Difficulty Level Taxonomy of Complex Triple Rhythm Patterns-Rests

Reading Recognition

Notational Understanding

Growth Rate Taxonomy of Complex Triple Rhythm Patterns-Rests

Reading Recognition

Notational Understanding

Difficulty Level Taxonomy of Complex Triple Rhythm Patterns-Ties

Aural Perception

Reading Recognition

Notational Understanding

Growth Rate Taxonomy of Complex Triple Rhythm Patterns-Ties

Aural Perception

Reading Recognition

Notational Understanding

Difficulty Level Taxonomy of Complex Triple Rhythm Patterns-Upbeats

Aural Perception

Reading Recognition

Growth Rate Taxonomy of Complex Triple Rhythm Patterns-Upbeats

Aural Perception

Reading Recognition

A SELECTED BIBLIOGRAPHY OF EXPERIMENTAL RESEARCH
STUDIES IN THE PSYCHOLOGY OF MUSIC FOR 1972

Arellano, Sonya I., and Draper, Jean E. "Relations Between Musical Aptitudes and Second-Language Learning." *Hispania* 55 (1972):111–121.

Bradley, Ian. "Effect on Student Musical Preference of a Listening Program in Contemporary Art Music." *Journal of Research in Music Education* 20 (1972): 344–353.

Buros, Oscar Krisen. *The Seventh Mental Measurements Yearbook*, Volumes 1 and 2. Highland Park, N.J.: Gryphon Press, 1972.

Cowden, Robert L. "A Comparison of First and Third Position Approaches to Violin Instruction." *Journal of Research in Music Education* 20 (1972):505–509.

Dawkins, Arthur, and Snyder, Robert. "Disadvantaged Junior High School Students Compared with Norms of Seashore Measures." *Journal of Research in Music Education* 20 (1972):438–444.

De Yarman, Robert M. "An Experimental Analysis of the Development of Rhythmic and Tonal Capabilities of Kindergarten and First Grade Children." In *Experimental Research in the Psychology of Music: 8*. Studies in the Psychology of Music, vol. 8. Iowa City: University of Iowa Press, 1972.

Duerksen, George L. "Some Effects of Expectation on Evaluation of Recorded Musical Performance." *Journal of Research in Music Education* 20 (1972): 268–279.

Edmonson, Frank A. "Effect of Interval Direction on Pitch Acuity in Solo Performance." *Journal of Research in Music Education* 20 (1972):246–254.

Franklin, Erik. *Music Education: Psychology and Method*. London: George G. Harrap and Co., 1972.

Gordon, Edwin. "Third-Year Results of a Five-Year Longitudinal Study of the Musical Achievement of Culturally-Disadvantaged Students." in *Experimental Research in the Psychology of Music: 8*. Studies in the Psychology of Music, vol. 8. Iowa City: University of Iowa Press, 1972.

Gregory, Thomas B. "The Effect of Rhythmic Notation Variables on Sight-Reading Errors." *Journal of Research in Music Education* 20 (1972):462–468.

Griffin, Lawrence R., and Eisenman, Russell. "Musical Ability and the Drake Musical Memory Test." *Educational and Psychological Measurement* 32 (1972):473–476.

Haack, Paul A. "Use of Positive and Negative Examples in Teaching the Concept of Musical Style." *Journal of Research in Music Education* 20 (1972):456–461.

Jeffries, Thomas B. "Familiarity-Frequency Ratings of Melodic Intervals." *Journal of Research in Music Education* 20 (1972):391–396.

Peretti, Peter. "A Study of Student Correlations Between Music and Six Paintings by Klee." *Journal of Research in Music Education* 20 (1972):501–504.

Reid, Charles R. "Relative Effectiveness of Contrasted Music Teaching Styles for the Culturally Deprived." *Journal of Research in Music Education* 20 (1972):484–490.

Schleuter, Stanley L. "An Investigation of the Interrelation of Personality Traits, Musical Aptitude, and Musical Achievement." In *Experimental Research in the Psychology of Music: 8.* Studies in the Psychology of Music, vol. 8. Iowa City: University of Iowa Press, 1972.

Siegel, Jane A. "The Nature of Absolute Pitch." In *Experimental Research in the Psychology of Music: 8.* Studies in the Psychology of Music, vol. 8. Iowa City: University of Iowa Press, 1972.

Smoliar, Stephen W. *A Parallel Processing Model of Musical Structures.* Cambridge, Mass.: Massachusetts Institute of Technology Artificial Intelligence Laboratory, 1972.

Thayer, Robert W. "The Interrelation of Personality Traits, Musical Achievement, and Different Measures of Musical Aptitude." In *Experimental Research in the Psychology of Music: 8.* Studies in the Psychology of Music, vol. 8. Iowa City: University of Iowa Press, 1972.

Webster, John C., Woodhead, M. M., and Carpenter, A. "Are Steady State Musical Sounds as Identifiable as Steady State Vowels?" In *Experimental Research in the Psychology of Music: 8.* Studies in the Psychology of Music, vol. 8. Iowa City: University of Iowa Press, 1972.

Williams, Robert O. "Effects of Musical Aptitude, Instruction, and Social Status on Attitudes Toward Music." *Journal of Research in Music Education* 20 (1972):362–369.

Yoder, Vance A. "A Study of Gaston's 'Test of Musicality' as Applied to College Students." *Journal of Research in Music Education* 20 (1972):491–495.

Young, William T. "A Statistical Comparison of Two Recent Musical Aptitude Tests." *Psychology in the Schools* 9 (1972):165–169.

Young, William T. "Musical Aptitude Profile Norms for Use with College and University Nonmusic Majors." *Journal of Research in Music Education* 20 (1972):385–390.

Zumbrunn, Karen. "A Guided Listening Program in Twentieth-Century Music for Junior High School Students." *Journal of Research in Music Education* 20 (1972):370–378.